The Ritter
Double-Cross

Frederick Nolan decided to be a writer very early in life but it
took him about 20 years to get round to it. Meanwhile he
acquired the necessary credentials for this biography by
working as a shipping clerk, carbon-paper salesman, electricity
showroom assistant, radio and TV salesman, GPO sorter,
squiggler in a chocolate factory. Unable to get a job as a
lumberjack (all the best authors at one time seemed to have
been lumberjacks), he co-founded what is now the English
Westerners Society, and wrote a definitive history of the
Lincoln County Wars in New Mexico. After a dozen years of
working for various publishers he co-founded in 1971 a
publishers' newsletter called *The Gee* Report and, as Frederick
H. Christian, found some success as a writer of westerns. He
now devotes himself full time to the study of the American
musical theatre, the life of Ernest Hemingway and writing.

By the same author

Frederick Nolan

The Ritter
Double-Cross

Futura Publications Limited
A Contact Book

A Contact Book

First published in Great Britain in 1974
by Arthur Barker Limited

First Futura publications edition 1976
published in association with Arthur Barker Ltd

ISBN 0 8600 7332 7

Printed in Great Britain by
Hazell Watson & Viney Ltd
Aylesbury, Bucks

Futura Publications Limited
110 Warner Road
Camberwell, London SE5

For Michael Meller
— the real Gee whizz

I

Chevalier supposed that he really ought to feel very honoured; but right at this moment, something like ten thousand feet above the very heart of the Third Reich, the honour of being the first non-RAF officer to fly in the prototype Manchester III bomber came a very bad second to his personal, and much more pressing need to stop his teeth from chattering like castanets. Even with the blankets draped around him and a full set of clothes beneath, the intense cold permeated every part of his body, numbing hands and feet, making him shiver with such intensity that the spasms threatened to jerk him right out of the makeshift canvas and metal seat rigged against the freezing metal struts of the bomber. Meanwhile the four new Merlin engines, each pulling at its top power of well over a thousand horsepower, thundered at a decibel level calculated to make Bedlam seem by comparison a quiet Eastbourne rest home for retired maiden ladies.

Deafened, frozen, his nerves as twang-tight as a guitar string, Major Paul Chevalier was in no mood to appreciate the many refinements of this new plane, although he had already filed the more important ones into his retentive memory.

Now he glanced quickly up at the pilot in his seat on the left-hand side of the cockpit, watching the young face with its luxuriant 'Flying Officer Kite' moustache intent on the battery of dials and gauges and clocks in front of him, their pale green glow casting an unearthly light in the darkened cockpit. You were getting old, they said, when the policemen started to look very young, but he knew it wasn't that which made him think of the pilot – and his crew, come to that – as kids. The RAF's losses in what was now being called 'the Battle of Britain' the preceding August had made heavy inroads into the ranks of its pilots, and the survivors, though young, were mostly seasoned veterans like this one, shouting terse asides to his flight engineer, totally immersed in flying the bucketing aircraft. If either of them noticed the blood-freezing cold, they gave no sign of it. The flight engineer clutched a clipboard firmly in his gauntleted hands, concentrating on what the pilot was telling him, making notes in indecipherable squiggles on the complicated-looking document in front of him, notes which would supply the boffins back in London with vital details of the prototype plane's performance.

They had been told before they took off that if all went well, the new bomber would go into production with a view to being Bomber Command's spearhead weapon in the coming months, carrying enough bombs to knock hell out of Hitler's war effort; but right now Chevalier would have traded all of the RAF's future planes for a stiff glass of Scotch. If the truth were told, he frankly didn't give a monkey's whether Wing Commander Johnson, his flight engineer, navigator, wireless operator and sergeant air-gunner ever got back to Britain or not. The whole wizard-pranging lot of them could nosedive right into the North Sea as far as Chevalier was concerned, as long as they first, flew him to the right place and second, dropped him and his four companions over the chosen area. The thought of what depended upon the accuracy of the Cockney navigator, hunched now in frowning concentration over his map table behind the pilot made him scowl, and he scrunched around in his seat, cursing as he banged his head against the parachute flares mounted on the metal wall of the fuselage, to look at the men who would accompany him on this mission.

Like himself, each of them was swaddled in heavy blue RAF blankets which didn't seem to be keeping any of them warmer than his own. Beneath the blankets, he knew, they were wearing civilian clothes such as any German working man might wear, and at their feet were the various satchels and fibreboard suitcases into which had been packed the accoutrements vital to the success of their operation.

Whitehead caught Chevalier's glance and grimaced, raising his eyes heavenward in that universally-recognized expression of patient suffering that also says 'Yes, but what can you do?' Chevalier tried for a grin, but the movement made his icy skin feel as if it might crack and he desisted.

Kenneth Whitehead – *Doctor* Kenneth Whitehead, he corrected himself – was a big man, perhaps six feet two or three, with wide shoulders and huge hands, the powerful frame of an athlete marrying strangely with his reputation as one of the top British research chemists.

Chevalier hoped fervently that the reputation was justified: Whitehead's knowledge would be almost as valuable as that of Captain George Davidson, a dour-faced Scot with a drooping moustache whose total expertise with any kind of explosive device would play a large part in their plans. Not the least of Davidson's additional talents was a virtuoso ability with guns, all of

3

which had resulted very early in the war in his being seconded to MO9 for 'special duties' which, Chevalier understood, consisted of training killer squads to raid German beach and harbour installations.

Next to Davidson sat W/O Mike 'Dusty' Miller, seconded to this operation from his normal duties as a maintenance engineer in one of the Government's hush-hush communications centres. He would be responsible for anything to do with electrical wiring, alarms, telephones; and also for transport, for Miller was, by inclination rather than profession, a motor car maniac. They said if you gave him four wheels and two pieces of wire, he could make something that could run on a pint of paraffin.

The last man in the party was Sergeant David Richardson who was, very simply, their radio man. He was a slightly-built, nervous-looking man with thinning blond hair and pale blue eyes which looked out apprehensively at the world through steel-rimmed glasses that had worn a ridge on the bridge of his rather long nose.

A mixed bag, Chevalier thought, but with the exception of Richardson, the very best he could have hoped for. All of them spoke fluent German, and all of them looked as nervous as hell. Chevalier grinned to himself. What a fine bunch of British fighting men, he thought. They sat huddled in the metal-framed canvas bucket seats, their breath billowing like steam to condense and freeze immediately on the vibrating metal panels, stamping their feet constantly, occasionally beating their arms across their chests in an effort to get some heat into their sluggish arteries; each man deep in his own thoughts, his own apprehensions, his own speculations about what lay ahead and beneath them.

The noise of the engines altered slightly, and the navigator reached around and back, banging on Chevalier's shoulder with a gloved fist.

'Twenty minutes!' he yelled.

He held up both hands with the fingers extended, closing them into fists then opening them wide again.

'Twenty minutes!' he shouted again, and Chevalier nodded, patting the navigator's outstretched arm to show he'd understood the message.

They would be over the drop zone in twenty minutes, and now his eyes moved to the taut metal wire which ran the length of the fuselage, along the metal ribbed walls with their naked, ugly spars dripping with freezing condensation. He toyed with the snap catch at the end of the line attached to his parachute, his mind far away ahead.

Then he turned and banged Whitehead on the shoulder.

'Hear that?' he yelled.

'I heard it,' Whitehead shouted back. 'Can't be soon enough for me!'

'Ever jumped before?'

'Only in training!'

If Whitehead was apprehensive about making his first parachute jump, he didn't show it. His eyes were positively a-gleam with anticipation, and he turned towards Davidson to pass on the news. Chevalier saw his mouth moving, but whatever words were used were lost in the monstrous roar of the huge Rolls-Royce Merlins as the pilot pushed the throttle forward and tilted the plane into a huge winging right hand bank that would take them on their final run south and east towards the target zone, Totes Moor, the Dead Marsh.

Miller shouted something that Chevalier couldn't hear.

'What?' he screeched.

'Looking forward . . . ,' Miller shouted. 'Clear night . . . stars.'

'What did he say?' Chevalier asked Whitehead.

'You won't believe it,' Whitehead said, his face close to Chevalier's to remove the need for shouting.

'What?'

'He said he's looking forward to the jump, because on a clear night you can see up to two thousand five hundred stars.'

'What?'

'That's right,' Whitehead grinned, leaning back to let Miller lean across Davidson's knees to shout something.

'Comes from reading comics since I was a nipper, Skip,' Miller said. 'You know, they always have that sort of "Believe it or Not" stuff printed in them. It's funny: I could always remember that, anything I read in them.'

'Really?' Chevalier said with a shrug.

Miller leaned back, a hurt expression on his open face.

'Bloody interlectuals,' he muttered to Davidson, who grinned.

Chevalier got up out of his seat and stood in the centre of the board walk running down the middle of the plane, rocking slightly with the movement of the aircraft. He made an exaggerated gesture of pointing at his watch.

'Synchronize!' he shouted.

They all nodded, and pushed back their sleeves, eyes on him as he said 'When I give the word, it will be 20.30 hours. Seven . . . six . . . five . . . .' Their faces were tense, expectant, the realization that action was imminent coming upon them simultaneously. 'Three ... two ... *mark*!' He nodded, and watched as they fumbled frozen-fingered with the winders of their watches.

'We jump at 20.45,' he shouted, lurching back to his bucket seat and huddling into the blankets.

'Cold, isn't it?' Whitehead shouted.

Chevalier nodded, concentrating again on keeping his teeth from breaking into another fandango. He didn't want to talk about the cold, or the weather, or anything.

'Makes you wish you was a land snail!' he heard Miller shout.

'I know I'm going to regret asking,' Whitehead yelled back, 'but why?'

'Man dies if his body temperature drops to 65 degrees Fahrenheit,' Miller bawled. 'Land snails can stay alive as low as minus 184 degrees.'

'They've got more sense than to jump out of aeroplanes, too!' was Davidson's dour rejoinder. 'You going to be spoutin' this rubbish all the time?'

'Nah,' Miller told him. 'Don't sound the same in German, somehow.'

'Good,' Davidson said, pulling his blankets tighter. 'Because Jerry hasn't got our tolerant sense of humour.'

'Well,' Miller said. 'From what we was told yesterday, I never thought they 'ad.'

Chevalier heard this last remark and nodded to himself. What they had been told yesterday had indeed been no laughing matter, and he let his mind drift back to the briefing room and what they had been told there.

He saw again the bilious green and cream painted brick walls with their blacked-out windows, the shaded green lights over the double wooden door beneath which came a biting, searching, foot-freezing draught. He remembered the village school of his own childhood as having been much like it, cramped desks with scarred, penknife-initialled tops, stone floors, the big blackboard with the bright lights focussed on it, the maps, the smell of chalk and wet clothes.

But this was no schoolroom. This was the Operations Room of RAF Bovingdon, a small airfield just north of Watford which, had the Luftwaffe been aware of it, presently contained enough top brass to fill Whitehall on Remembrance Sunday. He had arrived by car from London this grey and freezing January morning, having been given literally only six hours notice that the operation he had put up as a feasibility study was 'on' and that he would lead it. He had been escorted to the Officers' Mess, briefly introduced to his pilot and the four men who were to be his team. Their talk over the steaming tin mugs of NAAFI tea had been desultory, reticent, very English ; but Chevalier had been satisfied with the selection and delighted after he had been given their dossiers to read before the briefing.

It was growing dark by the time they were escorted to the Operations Room on the southern edge of the enclave, and they were given more tea by a dumpy WAAF who looked at them the way that Romans must have looked at gladiators. You couldn't keep such a flap a secret, not on a base as small as this. Everyone knew something was up, but Chevalier was quite certain that none of them had even the remotest idea of just how big that something was.

There were three men on the raised wooden dais at the front of the Operations Room, two in civilian clothes and the third in the uniform of a brigadier-general in the

8

army. Behind them on the wall was a huge 1 : 25,000 scale map of the Hanover area.

The five men exchanged glances but said nothing, sipping the scalding tea as the Brigadier-General rose to his feet and stood looking down at them.

'I'm sorry you men have been brought here with such lack of either ceremony or notice,' he began, 'but speed and secrecy were of the essence in this operation. Let me begin by saying that this briefing will be conducted on an entirely informal level, dispensing with the formalities of rank. You may smoke if you wish, ask questions whenever you feel you want to, and' – he permitted himself a slight smile – 'conduct yourselves as if each man in this room were the equal of the other.'

He paused for the forced smiles they pasted on their faces, and then hitched his rump on to the table.

'My name is Tunstall-Behrens, and I have been given the job of co-ordinating all aspects of this mission, with direct responsibility to the Prime Minister. I may add that he is taking a personal interest in it, for reasons which I shall explain. Let me say just this : the information which you are about to be given is of such a nature that if one word – one word, mind you – were to leak out and become public knowledge, we would have a national emergency of such proportions on our hands that it is entirely within the bounds of possibility that His Majesty's Government would be compelled to treat with Hitler for terms of surrender.'

2

If Brigadier-General Tunstall-Behrens had pulled the
pin of a Mills bomb and lobbed it among them, his
listeners could not have been more astonished, and they
stared back at the tall, thin soldier as he picked up a long
tapering wooden pointer and stepped back towards the
map on the wall. He tapped the map with the point.

'This is the town of Seelze. Village, really. Situated on
the north-western edge of Hanover, about thirteen
kilometres from the centre of the city. Seelze stands, as
you can see, close to a very important junction of vital
communications: the point at which the autobahn
routes cross, just north of Hanover, going east to Berlin,
north to Hamburg – well, you can see them for
yourselves – and also where the Mittellandkanal, a
major arterial waterway, forks to supply Hanover. In
addition to that, Seelze contains a major complex of
railway marshalling yards. All of which leads me to
believe that one of these days we'll be sending some of
our RAF chappies over there to flatten the place, but
that's not for this meeting. Our target is not the canal,
nor the motorway, nor even the marshalling yards. It is
in the town of Seelze itself.'

He unhitched the map of Germany and let it collapse
to the floor, pushing it aside with his foot as he concentrated upon the equally large-scale street map of the
centre of Seelze.

'Here, gentlemen, is the town of Seelze. It has no special features which attract the tourist, no mediaeval church or picturesque architecture. Seelze is an industrial suburb, and its main feature is the complex of factories which you see here on the western edge of the town. You will see that the Mittellandkanal and its branch, the Zweigkanal Linden, form the sides of a right-angled triangle whose base is the main street of Seelze – the Bahnhofstrasse. Parallel to the Zweigkanal Linden, which forms the vertical side of the triangle, is the main road to Hanover in the east, and the country town of Wunstorf in the west, which crosses the Mittellandkanal on the western edge of the town, and runs past the main station, the Hauptbahnhof, where it is joined – again at right angles – by the Bahnhofstrasse. Clear so far ?'

There were no queries, and Tunstall-Behrens nodded.

'On the northern side of the town, you can see the river Leine, which forms the effective edge of Seelze. Across this bridge at the northern end of the Bahnhofstrasse, the road makes an S-bend to join the Seelzer Landstrasse, leading to the town of Havelse und Garbsen, up here on the top right hand side.'

'The black and white dotted lines are . . . ?' Davidson began.

'The railway tracks, Captain,' Tunstall-Behrens anticipated. 'They run, as you can see, parallel to the Wunstorferstrasse, the main road I mentioned: Reichstrasse 441, to be precise. And now the factory complex. If you will open the envelopes on the desks in front of you, you will find some photographs inside. They are numbered one to five.'

The five men fumbled in the half-darkness with the brown manilla envelopes, ripping apart the wax seals and the heavy, red paper, 'Most Secret' labels plastered across every join, sliding the fan of 10 × 8 in. glossy prints on to their tables.

'The first photograph, gentlemen.'

It was a squat, two-storied building with a flat roof. There was an entrance at the left hand side, and over the doors they could see the words REIDEL U. DE HAEN in capitals, and then in smaller capitals beneath them SÜßSTOFFWERKE.

'*Saccharin* factory, sir ?' came Miller's surprised voice from the darkness.

'In a moment, Miller,' Tunstall-Behrens said. 'Photograph number two.'

The second photograph showed a smaller building, taken from a road across a patch of open ground. There was a high wire fence around, running across in front of it, and to one side they could see the sentry-controlled gateway with its diagonally striped sentry-box. There was a sign in German on the fence : the rigid eagle of the Third Reich clutching its swastika in its talons, and beneath it in huge capitals HOCHVERWALTUNG : EINTRITT, with some other message too blurred to read properly.

'The sign says "Halt at gate and show pass,"' Tunstall-Behrens explained. 'This is the main administration building. The first photo you saw was of the general administration building. Now photograph number three.'

The third photograph was a blurry but effective general view of the entire frontage of the complex, probably as seen from the Wunstorferstrasse. On the left they could see a maze of railway lines entering the complex alongside a huge block, behind which reared an even higher building. An alley ran between this and the general administration building, and behind that they could see two tall metal chimneys. As in the other photograph, the high wire fence with its board signs could be clearly seen running the entire length of the complex, broken only by sentry-controlled entrances barred by drop-poles similar to those used at frontier posts.

'The building on the left is the canteen barracks and dormitory for the guards – and let me tell you now that this complex is heavily guarded, gentlemen. Not only does it have a crack guard squad, which is changed every eight hours, but it also has a resident Gestapo staff. However, more of that later. Those chimneys, now. They are what we're really interested in. Let's look at the fourth and fifth pictures.'

These were really not much more than enlargements of snapshots. Taken from behind long grass, and distorted by having been shot at ground level, the pictures showed a wide, squarish white painted building from which what looked like a maze of piping ran to another brick building on the left of the picutre. The white building was airy and spacious looking, with a large proportion of its wall area given over to windows.

'That's our baby,' Tunstall-Behrens said, softly.

'What is it, sir?' asked Davidson.

'That's the laboratory, Captain,' the soldier said. 'And the *raison d'être* of this mission. You are going to Seelze to destroy it.'

'Begging the Brigadier-General's pardon,' Dusty Miller

put in, getting slowly to his feet. 'But why in the name of
. . . .' He hesitated, and Tunstall-Behrens smiled.

'I said informal and I meant it, Miller. Speak your
mind.'

'Well, I mean. What the hell are we doing blowing up
saccharine plants ?'

'A good question,' the officer replied. 'And I'll tell
you the answer. First, however, some background. In
1935, the Hanover company of J. Reidel and E. de Haen
built the factory you have just seen in those photographs,
as well as a sister-plant in the town of Leese, which is
about forty-five kilometres from Seelze, along
Reichstrasse 441. That's on the western side of the large
lake, the Steinhuder Meer, which you saw on the map.
The plant at Leese was designed originally as an
auxiliary to the one at Seelze, but it was never needed
and was turned over to the production of vanilla
flavouring and saccharin. To the best of our knowledge,
it still produces them. However, that is not the case where
the Seelze complex is concerned, as Major Chevalier's
people at SOE found out.'

He paused for a moment, taking a Player's Navy Cut
from the handsome silver cigarette case he carried in the
breast pocket of his immaculately cut tunic.

'Now let me tell you exactly who *Aktiengesellschaft
Reidel und de Haen* are. Or rather, were.'

He looked up to see that he had their full attention.
There was no question of it : they were watching him the
way a hypnotized bird watches a cobra.

'Reidel and de Haen, gentlemen, were the leading
manufacturers in Germany of chloracetophenone :
tear-gas, to you. At the outbreak of war, according to
Intelligence reports we have every reason to believe ac-

curate, they were stockpiling over one hundred tons of the stuff every month. Every month, gentlemen.'

'But . . . ,' Davidson started. The Brigadier-General held up his hand.

'I know,' he said. 'International treaties, the Hague Convention, all specifically excluded the use of gas in warfare. We all know that. In fact, were it only the manufacture of tear-gas, we would remain – relatively, at any rate – unperturbed. But the information we have is that something infinitely more sinister is going on at Seelze. To tell you more about it, Doctor Vernon Hunt of the Ministry of Defence has taken time off from his very valuable work in London to come here. Dr Hunt.'

He nodded at the slight, tubby man who was sitting at his right behind the paper-strewn table. Dr Hunt stood up, diffidence written all over his face, the expression of a man to whom any kind of public appearance is the sheerest torture. When he spoke, however, his voice was low-pitched and authoritative, and he had no difficulty in commanding their complete attention.

'Gentlemen,' Hunt said. 'I am afraid that what I am about to tell you will be a little difficult for you – as laymen – to comprehend. In the normal manner, I would suggest your taking notes, but in the present circumstances . . . .' He glanced at Tunstall-Behrens. 'No notes,' that worthy said flatly. 'Of any kind.'

'Of course,' Hunt said hastily. 'However, I shall do my best to simplify as I go along. The first thing I must do, therefore, is to give you a little historical background.' He smiled gently, as though asking their forgiveness for his personal indulgences. 'You will, of course, have heard that the Germans were the first to use gas in warfare – against the Russians on the Polish front in 1915, when they used chlorine gas. By the end of 1917, the use of mustard gas was fairly widespread. Indeed, some estimates put it that something like fifty per cent of all the shells fired by them were filled with some form of mustard gas. Fortunately for all of mankind, these weapons were crude and unreliable, and possessed of one great drawback : they could also be used in retaliation, for mustard gas is criminally easy to manufacture.'

'My understanding is that we used it ourselves,' Whitehead interposed.

'Doctor Davidson is quite right,' Hunt nodded, blinking rapidly. 'Although on a smaller scale – perhaps 20 per cent of our shells. It was this, we believe, which turned German thoughts towards the development of such weapons when Germany began to re-arm in the mid thirties. Assuming – rightly, I might add – that Britain had its own stockpile of such gases, the Germans began to search for even more formidable chemical warfare weapons. To do this, they called upon a brilliant research chemist from the University of Heidelberg, Dr Karl Heineman, whom they installed at the Reidel and de Haen plant in Seelze – in one of the most modern laboratories in Europe.'

'You will find in the folders on your desks a photograph of Dr Heineman – not a very good one, I'm afraid – together with a brief dossier on him. Read and memorize it,' Tunstall-Behrens told them.

'Let me explain something,' Hunt went on. 'The weapons we are talking about as gases, are not always in fact gases at all. Sometimes they are solid materials dispersed as a fine mist under pressure. However, the generic term 'gases' will suffice here.

'The Germans classified all their discoveries by colour

codes. Thus the simplest, least harmful gases like chloracetophonone or bromine acetic ester – irritant gases, mainly – were classified *Weisses Kreuz,* or White Cross.

'The next group, *Grünes Kreuz*, Green Cross, were the suffocating gases such as chlorine or phosgene, which attack the lungs; and the next in order of danger-level were the Blue Cross gases, like hydrid of arsenic and the cyanidic derivatives, which attack the oxygen in the blood and are almost always fatal unless the recipient can be brought clear of their effect and given massive amounts of oxygen.' *

The men in the well of the room listened, appalled, to the well-modulated, authoritative voice as it outlined this catalogue of horrors. When Tunstall-Behrens cleared his throat loudly, several of them jumped visibly.

'The last group was the Yellow Cross gases, or vesicants, such as mustard gas, which I have already mentioned, or a related compound known as nitrogen mustard. These are the disfiguring gases which burn the skin on contact, so we need not go into too much detail about their internal effect; I will leave it to your imaginations. So: those were the four major classified groups of gases, most of which are simple to manufacture and store. However, they all have one serious strategic drawback, or perhaps two. The first is that they are non-persistent. That is to say, because of their low density, they disperse rapidly when used, and of course, a change in the wind can have an effect the user may find unpleasant.' He allowed himself the briefest of brief smiles at his own colossal understatement. 'The second drawback was that the Germans were aware that all of these gases were also known to us, and that their use in battle would provoke massive and immediate retaliation. Yes.'

He nodded to himself as if someone had actually agreed with him, and took a sip from the water glass on the tin tray in front of him on the littered table.

'Now,' he said, 'we learn that Doctor Heineman is working on something at Seelze which makes the weapons about which I have just told you seem by comparison as dangerous as a child's toy pistol. That something is a group of gases, or compounds, so dangerous that they have not even been given a colour-cross classification. I am informed, and readily believe, that none but a very few top Nazis know of their existence. Before, however, I go into any more of my scientific double-talk' – he smiled at them forgivingly for not being scientists – 'you will hear from my good friend Doctor Robert Williams. Dr Williams is probably Britain's foremost researcher in neurological and related subjects. Listen very carefully to what he has to tell you. Doctor Williams?'

Williams was a short, lantern-jawed man of perhaps fifty, with heavy lines running from nose to mouth – a stubborn mouth with lips that made a straight line. He ran a hand through his thinning black hair, then rasped a thumb across his chin. He looked as if he hadn't shaved for forty-eight hours.

'Now,' he said. 'First of all, let met say that neurology is simply that which concerns the nerves, the nervous system, and only in so far as it involves any physical defect in that system. Everything else that may be wrong with your nerves should be referred to a psychiatrist.' He used the word the way a betrayed husband would use the word 'whore', and his listeners were surprised to detect in his voice the unmistakable nasal snarl of a Liverpool accent.

'The human body,' Williams went on, 'is a delicate and complex machine. As I'm sure you know, the brain gives the body orders through a nervous system which we might compare to a telephone exchange. Impulses are transmitted through what we might call, er, the communications network of the tissues. I could give you all this in seven-syllable words, but in a nutshell what happens is that the body produces a compound at the nerve junctions called acetyl choline. This compound is the most vital factor in the machinery which causes our bodies to work. Affect it in any way and the nervous system will collapse. Now in the normal way, the acetyl choline is removed – and the nerve restored to "ready-to-receive" again – by being broken down internally by an enzyme produced by the body for just this purpose. This enzyme is called cholinesterase. Yes, Sergeant?'

'Sorry, sir, but you've lost me,' Richardson said, hesitantly.

'Not surprised,' Williams replied brusquely. 'All right, look at it like this. Your brain is the telephone exchange. You put through a call to your right hand. "Pick up that book," you tell it. The phone rings, the hand answers, the order is transmitted, the book is picked up. Then the hand, so to speak, hangs up. The phone is ready to get the next message. Acetyle choline hears the message. Cholinesterase cancels it. Think of all that happening in the millionths of a second in which your body can activate the nerve impulse and you've got the basic idea. All clear?'

The listening men nodded in silence. What all this was

leading up to they did not yet know, but the very air was pregnant with the belief that, whatever it was, it was big – bigger than any of them could imagine. Just how big they were about to find out, because Williams now sat down abruptly, and Dr Hunt got to his feet again. This time he was puffing furiously on an old briar pipe. Whatever he was using for tobacco, it made Tunstall-Behrens wrinkle his nose as if someone had cracked a rotten egg directly under his patrician nostrils.

'Now, gentlemen,' Hunt began. 'Understanding a little of the mechanism of the human nervous system, you will begin to appreciate what might happen if a compound could be discovered which acted directly upon that miraculous enzyme that Dr Williams just told you about – cholinesterase.'

He nodded at the dawning comprehension on their faces.

'That's right, gentlemen,' he said softly. 'That's precisely right. Dr Heineman and his team at Seelze have discovered not one, but several such compounds. We call them nerve gases. They work by phosphorylating the cholinesterase in the . . . oh, dear, that will never do, will it?' He allowed himself another small smile, as if he, personally, rationed himself to one every hour or so. 'These, ah, gases. They add a chemical group to the enzyme which destroys it, or prevents its working properly. Very nasty.' He bent down, and from his briefcase he drew several large pieces of cardboard upon which those watching could discern large wording in coloured crayon.

'Now then,' Hunt said, holding up the first card. 'The first formula which the Heineman team came up with was a colourless liquid whose chemical name is cyanodimethylaminethoxphophine oxide. As you see from the card, they gave it the code-name *Tabun*. The name hung in the air like some awful shadow, but if he was aware of the effect his words were having, Hunt gave no sign.

'*Tabun,* however, was found to be only partially persistent,' Hunt went on cheerfully, 'so they went on with their researches, and came up with an improvement. This time the formula was fluoroisopropoxymethylphosphine oxide, or . . .' he held up his second board, '*Sarin.* This one was much more persistent, but still not the perfect, persistent, lethal combination that they wanted. We now hear that this compound has been perfected. The name of it is *Soman.*'

He held up the board with the word in red capitals glaring out at them, and let it sink in.

'*Soman,*' he said softly, 'the most deadly weapon that has ever been manufactured. When absorbed through eyes, nose or skin, death is inevitable. The higher the concentration, the faster the awful end. Within one or two minutes of exposure to it, any animal will die.'

'You'd better tell them the rest, Doctor,' Tunstall-Behrens said grimly. 'I want them to know exactly how important this is.'

'Very well,' Hunt said. 'I'm afraid it's rather unpleasant, but it's as well you understand. Earlier it was explained to you how these nerve gases act upon the human, or animal, nervous system. I want you now to visualize the following things happening over a period of not more than one hundred and twenty seconds. First there is an uncontrollable nasal drip, followed by a tightness in the chest which makes breathing extremely difficult. The vision becomes distorted, and severe breathing difficulties are encountered. Cramps, unchecked salivation, and massive perspiration, are followed by nausea, vomiting, involuntary urination and defecation, and then the collapse of the motor system. Control of limbs goes, spasmodic collapse follows. The subject then enters a coma, following which there is a huge bodily convulsion and then total cessation of breathing. Then death. In two minutes, gentlemen. At the most.'

'Thank you, Doctor,' Tunstall-Behrens said quietly, 'I think we'll have a short breather. Gentlemen, smoke if you wish.'

Dusty Miller's sigh was almost as loud as a gale in the stillness, and it brought nervous laughter which dissipated the wracking tension created by Dr Hunt's words. Miller scrabbled in his pocket for his Woodbines, feverishly lighting one and puffing on it as if his life depended on the action. If the others were slightly more leisurely in their reactions, they were no less stunned to silence by what they had been told.

'I imagine you knew about some of this,' Chevalier said to Whitehead. The big man smiled, shaking his head sadly.

'A little,' he admitted. 'But – my God, nothing like as much!'

Chevalier said nothing, his eyes withdrawn. 'Are they really so far ahead of us?'

'You did the feasibility study; you know already,' Whitehead said. 'They're miles ahead of us!'

Before either man could say more, Brigadier-General Tunstall-Behrens rapped on the table with his silver cigarette case to call their attention back to the matter at hand. He frowned down at the cigarette case, as though

22

just realizing what he had done with it.

'It will not come as any surprise to you to know now that your target is Seelze,' he said. 'However, there is more to it than a straightforward bit of fun and games with dynamite. You have already met your mission leader. Major Chevalier, would you now please come up here and outline your plans?'

Chevalier nodded, grinding out his cigarette in the upturned Cherry Blossom boot polish tin which served as an ashtray, and stepped into the bright circle of lights on the dais. His men turned expectant faces towards him. After the theory, the details. This was something they could get their teeth into, rather than the grim, but finally unbelievable horrors they had just heard about. The mind rejected ogres it could not conjure.

'Our mission,' Chevalier told them flatly, 'is three-tiered. One, we will attack and destroy the research laboratories at Seelze. Two, we will endeavour to locate and bring back as much research material connected with *Tabun, Sarin,* and especially *Soman,* as we can. And three, we will kidnap and bring back to England the man responsible for the whole programme – Dr Karl Heineman!'

Not one of them spoke. Each knew what his role was likely to be: Davidson the planning of the destruction of the factory – Whitehead the identification of the research material. The options were all too limited, anyway. They looked at Chevalier, waiting for his next words.

'All right,' he said harshly. 'Let's get down to details.'

3

So much to remember, Chevalier thought, and so little time to memorize it all. God knows, they must be desperate at the top. He corrected himself: they *were* desperate, and he knew why. Operation Sea-Lion, Hitler's grand strategy for the invasion of Britain, had been postponed in the autumn of 1940, but it seemed more than likely that it would be remounted – and launched – as soon as spring arrived. Even though the Luftwaffe had been flailed out of the skies over England by the RAF during the Battle of Britain, it was the only ray of sunshine in sight. Everywhere else, the war was going in Hitler's favour. Malta was under siege, the Straits of Messina virtually closed to the Allied convoys trying to reach the beleaguered, blitzkrieg'd island. Intelligence reports from Spain indicated every likelihood of Franco's adding his weight to the Axis alliance, thereby closing off the entire Mediterranean and the vital base at Gibraltar. British cities were being bombed nightly: London, Liverpool, Coventry, Southampton were rubbled wrecks of their former selves. The possibility that Hitler might use his new terror weapons, the nerve gases, in a possible Spring invasion had been too terrible to contemplate, and SOE had been given the word to come up with a feasibility study aimed at nullifying the German advantage in this field.

'In addition to all that,' Chevalier had told his men at the briefing, 'we're beginning to get whispers that Adolf plans to attack Russia in the spring. It's our belief that all of these developments are behind the hurry-up orders that Dr Heineman and his Seelze people have been given; Hitler wants to use the nerve gases against us, or the Russians, or both. So all the stops are being pulled out.'

'In fact,' Tunstall-Behrens had drawled, 'you chaps are being given the top-top red carpet treatment. The RAF is even providing a brand-new prototype bomber to get you where you're going faster than anything that ever flew so far into Germany before.'

'A prototype?' Davidson had asked. 'What's wrong with something tried and tested, Sir?' he added, as an afterthought.

'Well, I'm embroidering a bit, actually,' the Brigadier-General admitted. 'In point of fact, they want to try her out on a long run over the Ruhr – for range, altitude tests, things like that. Seemed a shame to waste the petrol, so you're going with her.'

'What kind of plane is it, sir?' Whitehead asked.

'Brand new Avro Manchester,' the soldier beamed.

'That's not a new plane,' Davidson protested. 'It's an old one. And a rotten one to boot, Sir.'

'Not this one, Captain,' their pilot, Wing Commander Johnson, had interposed, stroking his luxuriant moustache with a forefinger. 'She's an Avro special. Prototype BT308, fitted with Rolls Merlins.'

'I thought Manchesters had Vultures,' Miller said.

'They did, old son,' Johnson said. 'That's why Bristol Tango 308 is special. She'll climb at 250 feet a minute, and clock up 275 miles an hour with a full load.'

'You've flown her?' Chevalier asked.

''Course, old bean,' Johnson said, patting his shoulder reassuringly. 'She handles like a dream.'

He had left them then to get his own pre-flight instructions, and there had been time for a final word from Dr Hunt.

'You all understand that the only way to destroy these compounds is by fire?' he asked.

'We're using phosphorus grenades, Doctor,' Davidson said, almost reproachfully.

'Good, good,' Hunt said, in the tone of a man who wouldn't have known a phosphorus grenade from a bath towel. 'There's one final point I must make,' he added, looking at the Brigadier-General for permission.

'Fine, fine,' Tunstall-Behrens said, 'but hurry it along, won't you, Doctor? I want to buy these lads a drink in the Mess before they take off.'

'Very well,' Hunt said, his expression indicating that he didn't think particularly highly of the idea. 'Gentlemen, listen to me. You must not, under any imaginable circumstance, expose yourselves to the experimental areas in the laboratories. Everyone there wears protective clothing and gas masks. Once you have set your charges, get as far away from the place as you can. I think I told you about phosgene?'

They nodded, wondering what was going to come next.

'One of the Green Cross group,' Whitehead murmured, and Hunt looked at him like an approving headmaster.

'Right, right,' he said, nodding. 'Phosgene is one of the suffocators, and in sufficient intensity is a sure killer. Now, the danger of death from the compound *Sarin* is thirty times greater than the danger of death from phosgene. Three quarters of a milligram on the skin – say the equivalent of three grains of sand – will kill an adult in sixty seconds. The danger from *Soman* is therefore, by definition, incalculable. So take no chances. Handle nothing in that factory. Nothing.'

The two scientists had gone in a bustle of umbrellas, bowler hats, and dark coats, Hunt still stuffing papers into his overflowing briefcase, the very picture of the absent-minded professor. Chevalier had continued with the salient points of the briefing, re-iterating as often as he could, without making too big a song and dance about it, that the plan was entirely flexible, capable of being altered and adapted as necessary, for they could not know exactly what they would find at Seelze. Whitehead had one final question for Tunstall-Behrens.

'Yes, Major?' the Brigadier-General had said, raising his fine eyebrows slightly.

'Can I assume, as I have done all along, that the information we have about the plant and the programmes being worked on there, is reliable – I mean totally reliable?'

'You can,' the Brigadier-General said. 'A German officer whose specific duty is the security of the Seelze compound has a mistress in the town. She is a British agent.'

'I see, sir,' Whitehead said. 'Thank you.'

'Don't mention it,' Tunstall-Behrens said, and leaned back in his chair, watching without interrupting as Chevalier completed his briefing. They had all had their drink with him later in the Officer's Mess, but it had been a stilted and uncomfortable affair. The men were edgy, as strung up as racehorses at the starting gate.

Chevalier smiled at the memory of the dour Davidson bemoaning the fact that he didn't really want his whisky. He wouldn't have minded betting that Davidson would give ten pounds for his half-empty glass right now as they thundered through the blackness over Germany in the bucketing Manchester. 'Flies like a dream', he recalled the pilot boasting. He could see Johnson straining against the control column, fighting the machine as he dropped her into the soupy overcast and started to bank to port for the long turning-circle which would bring him over the drop zone.

'Jerry's quiet tonight!' yelled the navigator to the flight engineer, who grimaced at the words.

'Touch bloody wood, old boy!' he yelled back, his eyes on the pilot, busy correcting the tendency to stall when engine power was reduced. Without taking his eyes off the instruments, Johnson shouted at the top of his voice 'Three minutes!' and pressed a button on the control panel. A bell rang vibratingly through the body of the plane, and the sergeant/air-gunner standing by the fuselage door jumped, his body tensing, both hands falling ready on the lever which would open the door.

'Two minutes!' he shouted to them, holding up two fingers.

'Same to you, mate,' muttered Miller as the sergeant wrestled with the lever, using all his strength to open the door a few inches. The men sitting in the row of bucket seats along the raw metal wall tensed as the booming thunder of the engines was drowned by the screaming whistle of the slipstream. A seeking, icy wind immediately dropped the temperature inside the aircraft even further below freezing as the sergeant looked at Chevalier and nodded.

He stood up, stamping his feet and flexing cramped leg muscles that felt like blocks of wood. His hands were quite numb in the thin woollen gloves, but nothing showed on his face as the red light blinked on above the doorway, casting an eerie, bloody light across the faces of the men beside him. He reached up and slammed the cord clip hard on the taut jumping-wire, pulling against it to check that it was engaged, hearing the 'slackaslick' sounds as the others followed suit. Standing now in the full tearing pull of the slicing blizzard that was thrashing through the open doorway, flattening his clothes against his body as if they had been pasted on him, Chevalier gave a thumbs-up sign.

Dusty Miller lurched forward, hands holding desperately on to the ice-encrusted metal struts of the fuselage, his eyes fixed on the red light above the door as if it contained his salvation. He kept his eyes averted from the yawning maw of blackness beyond the doorway, partly because there were stinging slivers of ice on the edge of the roaring wind, and partly because he didn't want to look out into that empty, Stygian void until he had to. Miller edged forward until he was able to hold both sides of the doorway with hands already turned numb by the relentless cold, his face a strained, expressionless mask.

He turned his head back towards the others, trying for a grin, but as he did so the light turned green. The air-gunner slammed him on the back with a clenched fist and Miller, making a fingers-crossed gesture as he did so, hurled himself out into the whistling blackness. His body was torn away out of sight in a second, during which time Richardson was already in his place, poised, jumping, gone in a flurry of windmilling arms. One and then pause. Whitehead gone. One and then pause. Davidson gone. And then Chevalier was out through the doorway into the night as the sergeant/airgunner stood for a moment peering out, eyes slitted, as if he were able to see the bodies tumbling downwards towards the dark earth below. Then quickly he turned, lurching back towards the tail, banging his elbow on the metal struts of the fuselage and cursing as the pilot wheeled the plane in a tight turn. He hammered with the flat of his hand on the makeshift folding door which screened off the rear gun-turret.

After a moment the door opened, and a figure in a bulky kapok survival-suit crawled through the aperture on hands and knees, dragging a parachute pack behind him.

'Come on, come on!' the sergeant shouted. 'We 'aven't got all bloody night!'

The man who had come through the aperture managed to get to his feet, steadying himself with one hand against the side of the plane. The floor was now tilted at an angle of about 45 degrees and he had difficulty in keeping his balance.

'Sorry!' he shouted. 'I damned near froze to death back there!' His voice was deep and strong but the sergeant/airgunner, whose name was Nolan and who came from Belfast, had no time to notice it. All he noticed was that the mysterious extra passenger was too tall to stand upright inside the plane at this point – which made him well over six feet – and that the man was catastrophically ugly, with a face, as Sergeant Nolan put it later, like a broken packing-case. Together the two men stumbled towards the still-open doorway, recoiling from the enormous, howling blast coming in through it.

The red light was on again, and even as the big man straightened fully, stamping his feet as he snapped the parachute cord clip on to the jumping-wire, it changed to green.

'Go, go, go, go, go!' screeched Sergeant Nolan, banging the big man in the small of the back. He saw the head move, as if in a nod, and then the man was gone out into the blackness. The sergeant rushed hastily to the rear of the plane again, dragging two large tubular canisters with attached parachutes, cursing and sweating even in this intense cold as he manhandled them to the doorway and shoved them unceremoniously out into the darkness, the cords tautening, jerking, and then blowing free and loose as the 'chutes opened way below.

With a huge effort somewhere between desperation and relief, the sergeant slammed the heavy door shut, every fibre of his body begging for warmth. With the roaring slipstream cut off, the frozen interior of the plane seemed almost friendly by comparison, and he staggered up forward, banging against the partition to the navigator's compartment. 'All away!' he panted, his mouth slack with effort. 'All away!'

'All right, skipper!' the navigator yelled. 'Let's go home!'

'Right you are!' Johnson shouted back, shoving the throttles up to full boost. 'Put the kettle on, Freddy!'

Sergeant/air-gunner Nolan's reply was – perhaps fortunately for him – lost in the surging roar of the quadruple Merlins at full power, and the big plane wheeled like some strange prehistoric bird in the starless darkness.

Far, far below, the first man was just landing on the soft, yielding ice-covered surface of the Totes Moor.

4

The drop had been almost perfect. Whatever you said about his flying – and Davidson had said quite a few things, none of them complimentary, while he'd been getting bruised and battered in the tossing Manchester – Wing Commander Johnson had gauged the drop beautifully. As he skimmed across the night sky, feeling that strange exhilaration that comes as the 'chute bears you weightless, formless, unseen, like some twentieth-century angel suspended between heaven and earth, Davidson caught the faint phosphorescent glimmer of the Steinhuder Meer far below. Then suddenly he saw the ground coming up at him fast, and he reached up quickly into the lines, yanking himself upwards and at the same time raising and bending his knees to lessen the impact of landing – the classic parachutist's landing position. He might as well not have bothered. The ground was soft, spongy, covered in a thin layer of skim ice that crackled alarmingly as Davidson's feet hit and dragged slightly, throwing him face forward into the chilly slime. Cursing, pawing the muck off his face, Davidson got to his feet as the chute billowed down, the wind at ground level no more than a breeze that kept the lines tugging gently at the shoulder straps. He hauled the 'chute in, cursing the soggy wetness beneath his feet that made it necessary to keep shifting stance or sink to the ankles in the waterlogged loam. Rolling the parachute into as tight a bundle as possible, he laid it on the ground and started stamping it into the mud, stamping and stamping and stamping of the frail silk until he was out of breath and the parachute was a torn and muddy mess already several inches below the normal level of the ground. Davidson stepped away from it, knowing that the boggy mud would soon seep back and cover the chute completely. Unless someone actually stepped on it, it would never be found. And it was hardly likely that anyone would do that.

Davidson knew from the hours he had spent studying the pre-war Lower Saxony *Landesverwaltungsamt* survey maps that the Totes Moor was a peat marsh, crisscrossed by footpaths and work roads which ran along raised embankments that also acted as dams. It spread like a bulging sunbonnet set on the back-tilted head of the Steinhuder Meer, to the edge of the village of Eilvese in the north, to Steinhude in the south, and to Neustadt am Rubenberge in the east. This, the largest town in the area was, as its name implied, a centre for the farmers of the region. The nearest habitation was at Eilvese, about four kilometres away. The Dead Marsh was quite simply a producer of peat, empty most of the time except for the waders and other sea birds, the rising chatter of whose querulous alarm formed a strangely soothing background noise. He checked his small compass, found that he was facing north. He knew from memory that this meant he was looking towards a forested area of rolling hills rising to a hundred and fifty feet or so.

He fumbled in his pocket for the hooded, rubber-cased torch and with economical precision flashed it three times to each of the major points of the compass. After a moment, he heard movement, and the sound of someone squelching into wetness, muffling an explosive curse of anger. Whitehead loomed blacker than the blackness of the night, teeth chattering with cold. He had stepped into a peat hole and his trousers were soaked to the knees.

'You all right?' Davidson asked urgently, pitching his voice low so that it would not carry.

'All right,' Whitehead hissed, unwilling to open his mouth any more lest the chattering of his teeth become uncontrollable. They stood waiting, and after a few more minutes Miller appeared, limping slightly from a heavy landing, his arm around the shoulder of Chevalier, whose face was streaked with mud.

'It's all right,' Miller said, holding up a hand when he could at last see the expression on Davidson's face. 'Just twisted me ankle. Be right as rain in a jiff.'

'Any of you see Richardson?' Chevalier asked.

'He jumped in front of me,' Davidson told them. 'All arms and legs. You think he got down okay?'

'Never seen him come down,' Miller said. ''Course, that doesn't mean nothing.'

'Damn!' Chevalier rasped. 'We'll have to try and find him. Spread out and use your torches. As long as you keep them down, no one will see them out here.'

'Watch out for birds' nest,' Davidson warned. 'These bloody birds can give you heart failure if they fly up in your face.'

As if in mocking echo of his words they heard a curlew weepy-weep-weeping somewhere like the ghost of a blackbird.

'Let's go,' Chevalier said, and they moved forward across the drop line.

As they moved, they spread slightly outwards, away

from each other, in a fan, the tiny torchlights bobbing like a line of fireflies as they stumbled and slithered in the muddy turf, cursing at the seabirds that fled in shrieking alarm at their approach.

Miller found him.

His low, urgent shout brought the rest of them at a precipitant run to where the little man stood over Richardson's sprawled form, his torch shining on the ghastly, sightless eyes of the radio operator. Richardson's head was twisted impossibly to the right, the rimless spectacles hanging askew from one ear. There was an astonished expression on his face. Davidson bent quickly down beside the body, feeling for a heartbeat beneath the waterlogged clothes. He shook his head.

'Dead,' he said. 'I think his neck is broken.'

'How in the name of God . . . ?' Whitehead began.

'It can happen,' Chevalier said, grimly. 'Look at the way the lines of his chute are tangled. He must have landed badly.'

'On ground as soft as this?' Davidson argued. 'He'd have had to land on his head at forty miles an hour to . . . .'

'Listen to me!' Chevalier snapped. 'He could have hit a stone, a peat stack, anything. It doesn't really matter – he's just as dead. Our main concern is not how it happened, but the fact that it did. Now – get that radio pack off his back, Miller, and check it out. You others scout around and see if you can find anything to dig with. There must be some shovels somewhere.'

Miller bent down and wrestled with the webbing straps holding the bulky haversack containing the radio, grimacing with distate as the dead man's head lolled obscenely.

'Give us a hand, mate,' he said to Chevalier, who

nodded and held the rapidly stiffening body as Miller tugged the satchel away. Davidson and Whitehead came back out of the darkness. They had found a rusty old spade leaning against one of the big stacks of cut peat.

'Get digging,' Chevalier said. 'We've still got to find our supplies.'

Miller looked up, surprised at the harshness in Chevalier's voice, but he made no comment, just looked at Davidson and shrugged.

'What about that radio ?' Davidson said.

'Nothing yet,' Miller said.

'Never mind, you can do that later,' Chevalier said. 'Miller, you and Whitehead take care of Richardson's body. We –' he jerked his head towards Davidson – 'will see if we can round up the rest of our stuff.'

'I 'ope you 'ave more luck than I'm 'avin' with this blasted thing,' Miller grumbled gloomily. He pushed the radio pack aside, jamming the aerial down into its socket and fastening the canvas flaps, as Chevalier and Davidson slopped away into the darkness. Heaving a sigh, he got to his feet and went over to help Whitehead.

By midnight they had found a woodsman's hut on the edge of the Schneerenwald, the pine forest on the northern edge of the Dead Marsh. It was a rude and simple wooden shack, its sagging door hinged with rotting leather. An empty glassless hole served as a window. It was closed by a wooden board on leather hinges as rotten as those of the door, which dropped down and hung more or less squarely over the aperture. They hung one of the blankets over the window to make sure that no light showed outside, another two at the door. These precautions also effectively sealed off most of the draught, so that by the time Miller's little primus stove had been hissing for a while, the atmosphere was thick enough to cut with a knife. Compounded of the combined smells of wet wool, rubber boots, drying bodies, beef tea and the meaty mess Miller was presently stirring in a flat tin pan on the primus, the air inside the hut would have offended a badger but none of the men complained. The pure, blessed relief of warmth and food rendered it sweeter to them than honeysuckle on an autumn evening, and they sat hunched around the stove, tin cups steaming in their hands, sipping the scalding Bovril as much for warmth as for sustenance. Their supplies were piled in the far corner of the room, alongside the shovels and cutting hoes stored here by the woodsmen and peat-cutters. There had been very little conversation since they had completed the doleful task of burying Sergeant Richardson and lugged their supplies into the hut.

'Come on with that food, Dusty,' Davidson said. 'I'm starving.'

'All right, all right,' Miller said. 'I'm doin' me best.'

'What is it, anyway?' Whitehead asked, more to make a sound than out of any real interest. The heavy double weight of fatigue and worry was pressing on all of them since Miller had announced, with terrible finality, that the radio was completely useless and that until he could scrounge some 'bits and pieces', as he called them, there was no way he could even try to fix it.

'It's called knock-knock,' Miller said, trying for a grin which didn't quite make it.

'What?' asked Davidson.

'Knock-knock,' Miller said, persisting. 'Go on, say it.'

'Jesus,' Davidson replied. 'You mean "who's there?"' there?"'

'S'right,' Dusty said. 'Irish stew.'

'Irish stew?'

'Irish stew in the name of the Lor,' Miller said, looking from face to face for signs of a response to the tired joke.

'Oh, Lord,' Whitehead said, wearily.

'Well,' Miller said, defensively, drawing the word out. His face brightened as something else occurred to him. 'We should've all been bedbugs,' he said.

'Dusty,' Davidson said, warningly.

'S'true,' Miller said, scooping stew and pouring it on to tin plates as he spoke. 'A bedbug can go 565 days without food.'

'Aye, and if this was what he was being offered, I can't say I'd blame him,' growled Davidson. He looked at the greasy mess on the plate without much enthusiasm, poking at it with the tin fork.

'Eat,' Chevalier said, taking his plate from Miller. 'We don't know when we'll get our next meal and we'll need all our strength.'

They ate in a silence broken only by the scraping of their forks on the plates, wolfing down the food in spite of their pretended distaste.

'Aaah,' Miller said, leaning back against his rucksack. He fished into his pocket for a cigarette and lit it by leaning forward and poking it into the flame of the little stove.

'Enjoy that,' Chevalier said. 'It'll be your last for a while.'

'Eh?' Miller said, sitting up.

'You don't think you can pull out a packet of Woodbines and offer them round on the train, do you?' Chevalier asked sarcastically.

'Blimey,' Miller said. 'I forgot about that.'

'It's the little things that catch you out,' Chevalier said. 'So from now on, we speak only German, think German, act German. *Verstanden?*'

'Understood,' Whitehead replied.

'No!' snapped Chevalier. 'German. Nothing else. No jokes, no whispers, not one word more of English!'

'He's right!' Davidson confirmed, speaking German now. 'One of the oldest interrogation techniques is to conduct the entire thing in one language, and then, somewhere, to throw in a casual phrase in the suspected mother tongue – something like "Do you smoke?" If you reach for the cigarette, you're finished. So watch it.' He turned to Chevalier. 'We'd better start thinking about getting some sleep soon,' he said. 'You'll want to hold the briefing first.' Chevalier nodded. His eyes were red with strain and there were deep lines of tiredness around his mouth. He reached into his satchel and withdrew the large-scale map of the area, spreading it on the floor. Miller brought the candles over and they spilled grease on the floor, setting the candles upright in the puddles so that they cast maximum light on the chart.

'Pay close attention now,' Chevalier said. 'Because we won't be able to use this map after tonight – workmen would look pretty silly referring to an ordnance map to get from their home to work.'

He pointed at the green patch in the upper left hand corner.

'This is where we are, in the Schneerenwald,' he told them. 'That H just there is this hut. You'll see the whole wood is shaped a bit like Wales, with us sort of near Cardiff. Up in the centre – about Aberystwyth – the road cuts through the woods, going west to the town of Schneeren from which the woods take their name. On the north-western edge of the woods is the main road between Bremen and Hanover – Reichstrasse 6 – and you can see that the Schneeren road joins it . . . here. Directly opposite is an unmade road – if you followed it right through it would bring you to Eilvese. Now here' – he traced the road and stopped halfway along, the point of his sheath-knife indicating a tiny red line with a dot at the end of it – 'there's a path (the red line) leading to a hay barn (the dot). Inside the barn will be four bicycles.'

'How the . . . ?' Whitehead ejaculated. Chevalier held up a hand, smiling.

'It's been laid on, courtesy of SOE,' he said. 'We've got our contacts – all over Germany. Four bikes will be there. Or rather,' he amended grimly, 'they'd better be, or we're in for a long hike. There will also be four largeish rucksacks, fairly battered specimens, into which we'll transfer our vital equipment. Everything else will be abandoned. We won't be needing it after tomorrow morning.'

'When do we move out?' Miller wanted to know.

'We leave here before dawn in pairs,' Chevalier said. 'You'll go first, with Davidson. Whitehead and myself will follow fifteen minutes later. Now look at this map again. You take this footpath that runs past the hut through the woods, up past this waterworks here, and on to the dirt road. Turn right when you reach it, and you'll come to the Bremen road, here. It's about a half-mile walk. Across the Reichstrasse, into the barn, get your bikes, ditch your equipment, return to the main road. Follow it south-west to the junction – here, at Himmelreich. Then take the road south to Neustadt – not the Reichstrasse, but the local road. It leads directly into the centre of Neustadt. By the time you get there, it should be close to seven-thirty. The streets will be full of people going to work, so nobody's going to take any notice of four more. Rendezvous at the Hauptbahnhof – the main railroad station, here just to the right of the crossroads in the centre of Neustadt – at 07.45. If you're not there, or we don't turn up by that time, the mission is aborted and each man tries to make his own way home the best way he can. Understood?'

There were solemn nods to show that everyone clearly understood. From the moment they set foot outside this hut in the morning they would all be at maximum risk, and would remain at maximum risk until their mission was completed and they were out of Germany again.

'What happens after we rendezvous at Neustadt?' Whitehead asked.

'There are trains to Hanover from there,' Chevalier explained. 'They pick up factory workers going to the city from the smaller towns, stopping all the way down the line. You can see it on the map: Neustadt to Poggenhagen, then south again to Wunstorf where the line bears sharp west to Gümmer, Lohnde, and Seelze. Which is where we get off,' he finished, with a slight smile.

'It sounds too easy,' Davidson said, reluctantly.

'I suppose it does really,' Chevalier replied. 'And in fact, it is. We just buy our tickets and get on the train. There's no reason to suppose we'll have any trouble, and our papers have been prepared by the best forgers in Q section. If anyone had any idea that we were here, these woods would be rotten with German soldiers and dogs baying for our blood. The fact that they aren't suggests we're all right so far, and four workmen on their way to Seelze shouldn't attract any attention. That part ought to be relatively easy.'

'If it is,' Miller said feelingly, 'it'll be the first part of this op. that has been.' He kicked the canvas container with the radio in it. 'If only I could strip this bitch down and spend a couple of hours on her.'

'There's not going to be time for that,' Chevalier said, quickly. 'We're just going to have to dispense with radio contact, and trust London to deliver the goods when it's time for us to get out.'

'I suppose you're right,' Davidson agreed, reluctantly. 'But I hate like hell just abandoning the radio.'

'So do I,' Chevalier agreed. 'So does everyone, I'm sure. But it's just so much excess baggage unless we can get whatever Dusty needs to fix it – and he doesn't know what that is until he's had a chance to strip it down.'

'I could have a go now, Skipper,' Miller said. 'If I took first watch.'

'Fair enough,' Chevalier said. 'One and a half hours, Dusty. Then you wake me and I'll take the next watch. And so on.'

Miller nodded and dragged the transmitter into the square of light cast by the four candles as the rest of them unrolled their sleeping bags and wormed into them.

'Sleep,' Davidson muttered. 'Who can sleep?'

He kicked the sleeping bag into shape, crawling into it with muttered grumbles about cold, and damp, and the impossibility of sleeping surrounded by the entire Wehrmacht in the boggy middle of bloody Germany. The others grinned as they pulled the flaps over their faces and tried to find a soft spot on the rough earthen floor. Ten minutes later, there wasn't a sound in the hut except the faint metallic sounds of Miller's penknife tinkering with the insides of the radio, and the long rolling susurration of George Davidson's snores.

5

The first faint pink-grey streaks of approaching dawn were touching the sky to the west as Chevalier and Whitehead trudged through the dripping, gloomy woods along the footpath leading to the waterworks. There was a chill breeze this morning, coming fresh off the Steinhuder Meer, and bringing the faint hint of the sea with it. There were squirrels skittering about in the undergrowth and Whitehead remarked on it.

'No, they don't hibernate,' Chevalier said. 'People think they do, but they don't. They're not active much of the day, though.'

'You a country boy, Paul?'

Chevalier nodded.

'How did you get into this?'

'This business, or this particular job?'

'Whichever you like,' Whitehead said.

They walked awhile in silence, the thick carpet of pine needles totally muffling the sound of their footsteps. Somewhere in the high branches of the pines they heard a bird flap noisily away in panic, but apart from that the woods were still and eerie, and they could have been forgiven for believing that they were the last men alive on earth.

'It's a long story,' Chevalier said reluctantly.

'It's a long walk,' Whitehead pointed out.

They trudged on for a little longer, the footpath curving gently to the left all the while. Chevalier began to talk, choosing his words carefully, as if he was concerned to get each phrase exactly right.

'I'm with SOE,' he said. 'You know what that is?'

'Vaguely, from the briefings.'

'It's a branch of the secret service. Special Operations such as subversion, sabotage, political warfare. We call it "the old firm".'

'Where are you based?'

'Oh, our people are scattered all over the place. I was with SO3, which is at 64, Baker Street, Norgeby House. I was co-opted when the war broke out.'

'Oh,' Whitehead said, a slight hint of a question in the sound.

'I was in the BBC Foreign Service,' Chevalier said. 'Then when SOE was formed, I was drafted in. Hugh Dalton interviewed me personally.'

'Did you go into the BBC straight from ...?' Whitehead let the next question dangle, the way Englishmen will. Chevalier ignored it.

'You don't understand,' he said impatiently. 'I was living in Germany until the end of 1937. My mother was German, my father French. If you can call Alsace French.' He smiled mirthlessly. 'They used to say Alsace had changed hands more times than a seventy-year-old whore.'

'What happened?'

'Well, when the Nazis came to power, it was obvious what would happen next. My father would be called to serve in the Wehrmacht. He was a good German, the old fashioned kind, not one of those National Socialist rats. So we fled to France, and from there across to England. I was lucky – speaking French, German, and English, I hadn't much trouble getting work.'

'And then SOE.'

'That's right. Sifting intelligence reports, and running a team of agents in the field after a while. But it's no way to fight a war. I wanted to see real action. So I volunteered, as soon as I heard that my feasibility study had been accepted, to lead this mission. And they accepted me.'

'Do you know this part of Germany well? You seem to.'

'Not personally. We lived in Frankfurt. Do you know Frankfurt?'

'Not at all.'

'We lived in a nice apartment on the Bergerstrasse. No, I know this section through running agents here.'

'How many of them are there?'

'Only two at the moment. We've been having bad luck. Jerry has picked up three of my people over the last month or so.'

'Did you pick this team yourself?'

'No,' Chevalier said. 'That was done by the higher-ups: Gladwyn Jebb, Dalton, Gaitskell, some special representative of Churchill's. All I did was to stipulate what kind of expertise I wanted – they did the rest. Then I read all your dossiers, of course.'

'No need to tell you my life-story, then,' Whitehead said.

'Why not?' Chevalier said, disarmingly. 'Your work must be interesting. And dangerous, I imagine.'

'Interesting, yes. Dangerous, hardly ever,' Whitehead replied. 'We're not inclined to take risks in my line of work.'

'You're Ministry of Supply?'

'Officially, yes. Actually Porton Down is a research centre. Much the same as the one at Seelze, I imagine.'

'You were working on the same kind of projects?'

'Among other things. But we're nowhere near as far ahead as Heineman seems to be. Which is why I'm here.'

'Well,' Chevalier said. 'I asked for an expert, and I assume that's what you are. You've enough letters after your name.'

'I got most of those at Cambridge,' Whitehead smiled. 'But I think I know enough to find what we're looking for – if it's there.'

'It's there,' Chevalier said gruffly. 'It's there.'

They emerged now into an open clearing. The pine trees had been felled over an area of about a hundred square metres, and off to one side beyond it were a group of stone buildings. They took to the trees on the right hand side of the footpath, skirting around the clearing until they were on the far side. There was no sign of activity in the buildings.

'That's the waterworks,' Chevalier panted. 'Just a well and a pumping station, to clear drainage ditches.' He jerked a thumb in the direction of the woods behind them, and now Whitehead could hear the trickle of the water.

They pushed on ahead through the tangled undergrowth, brambles tearing at their legs, until they came back on to the pathway. About fifty yards ahead they could see the wider logging road crossing the footpath at right angles.

'Almost there,' Chevalier said.

They came out of the woods on to the wider road, rutted from the passage of tractors and log-trailers, the tracks half-frozen into a jumbled mess of torn earth and muddy puddles. There were two huge piles of stripped logs laid alongside the roadway awaiting transportation, and they turned right now, going downhill slightly towards the wide ribbon of the Reichsstrasse which they could see through the thinning trees ahead. Within ten minutes, they were standing on the fringe of the forest. Across the road they could see the open dirt road and off, about half a mile away, the white boxes of the houses in Eilvese, sprinkled like a child's building blocks on the side of the gentle hill, crowned with pines, to the northeast of the village.

They started forward, and were out in the open near the edge of the road, when Whitehead suddenly grabbed Chevalier's arm and pulled him back and around, pivoting on his heels and hurling the smaller man the way a hammer-thrower releases the hammer, across the torn tyre-tracks and behind an uneven pile of lumber stacked at the edge of the trees. Chevalier landed sprawling in an ungainly heap, smacking his head against the logs, his mouth a round O of astonishment, the breath driven from his unsuspecting body. He watched helplessly as Whitehead came across the open ground in a long, diving run, landing almost on top of him as he leaped for the shelter of the logs, and flattened out in the dirt alongside him.

'Get your head down!' Whitehead hissed, and Chevalier ducked instinctively as, in the same moment, the faint sound which Whitehead's acute hearing had detected, became a drone and then a solid roar. Then two army trucks, loaded with German troops in long grey greatcoats, roared past their hiding place and down the road towards Neustadt.

'They're up bright and early,' muttered Whitehead,

48

waiting a moment or two longer before he got slowly to his feet, brushing the matted loam and clinging leaves from his clothing. 'Come on, they've gone.'

Chevalier got to his feet carefully, like a man expecting to find bones broken, a puzzled look on his face as he regarded Whitehead.

'You're pretty athletic – for a scientist,' he remarked.

'Squash,' the big man replied.

'Eh?'

'Squash,' Whitehead repeated. 'It's our only vice. At work. We play squash every chance we get. It's a hard game – but it keeps you in shape.'

'It does that,' Chevalier said sourly.

'*Mens sana in corpore sano,*' Whitehead told him, but Chevalier just grunted, a sound that might have meant anything from agreement to disgust, and without further ado led the way across the wide concrete ribbon of the Bremen road at a brisk trot. Five minutes later they were outside the barn, and in another ten their unwanted rubber boots, sleeping bags, plates and other gear were buried in a deep hole beneath a shelving loam bank at the back of the dilapidated wooden building, covered with loose earth and leaves that made them invisible from three feet away. Wobbling slightly, suitcases strapped on to the panniers behind them, the two men cycled out on to the Reichsstrasse which stretched grey and flat and empty in front of them.

'Cor!' Dusty Miller breathed.

They were standing in the forecourt of the railway station in Neustadt, their bicycles already slotted into the rack opposite the newspaper kiosk. Davidson was reading – or pretending to read, Miller didn't know which – a *Völkischer Beobachter*. How anyone could read that old Germanic script Miller neither knew nor cared, for his wide eyes were fixed upon a burly working man in blue overalls who had just come out of the Bahnhof-buffet. In his meaty hand the man held a thick, juicy sausage into which he bit with obvious relish, taking a bite immediately afterwards from the bread roll in his other hand. The sausage steamed in the cold air, and Dusty felt the saliva spring to fill his mouth. The man took another lusty bite at his snack.

'Cor! Miller said again, and with a jerk of the head, indicated to Davidson that he was going in to get himself one. Before Davidson could frame an objection, the little man was gone, up the steps and into the restaurant from which he emerged several minutes later with a triumphant grin. His right and left hands each held a steaming *Wurst,* and he had several bread rolls stuck in his jacket pocket. He crossed the busy forecourt, ignoring the grins of workers passing him on their way into the station, and handed one to Davidson with a mock bow.

'*Guten Appetit, mein Herr,*' Miller said.

'*Viel, vielen Dank,*' Davidson grinned in reply.

The *Bratwurst* tasted marvellous as they stood there in the faint drizzle waiting. It was a cold, grey, blustery day now. The wind had freshened as they had cycled along the long straight road into Neustadt, down the slight slope, beneath the railway bridge that crossed the road and into the Hannoverschestrasse and the centre of the town, crowded with blue-overalled cyclists, women in trousers, with their hair tied back in severe buns, bustling along the pavements, children on their way to school swinging satchels.

'We turn right just after the cemetery,' Davidson shouted over his shoulder. Somewhere ahead they could hear a church clock striking the half hour, and they came to a halt at the crowded crossroads controlled by a traffic policeman in his shiny shako hat, grey cape damp and heavy on his shoulders and a bored, sightless expression on his face. A tramcar came clanging down the street, warning aside the thronging cyclists clustered in its tracks, who paid not the slightest attention to the irritated driver's noise. Army trucks roared by, dipping their noses to disappear beneath the iron bridge crossing the Huttendammstrasse. The station was about fifty yards along on their right, and another policeman, equally uninterested in the passers-by, was directing the constant flow of pedestrians into the station forecourt. Everywhere they saw the grey uniforms of the Wehrmacht and once or twice saw the *Sigrunen* of the SS on the helmets and collars of passing soldiers.

At twenty to eight, Davidson spotted Chevalier and Whitehead wheeling their bikes across the Huttendammstrasse into the station forecourt, and gestured with his chin towards the cycle rack. Chevalier nodded almost imperceptibly and wheeled his machine towards the rack, with Whitehead at his heels. The bigger man's cheeks were flushed from the cold and the exertion. They came over to where Davidson and Miller stood, and Chevalier said 'Two at a time.'

Davidson nodded, and he and Miller went ahead into the station, getting in line behind the men waiting to buy tickets, leaving their battered rucksacks on the platform behind them, where Chevalier could keep an eye on them.

'Return, Seelze,' Davidson told the ticket clerk.

'Four marks,' was the uninterested reply. The man didn't even look up as Davidson paid over his money and Miller took his place. They returned to their cases as Whitehead and Chevalier placed their own suitcases alongside the other two and joined the line. When they had their tickets, they went into the passageway and beneath the lines, up the stairs on the far side. There was a clock face hung on one of the uprights supporting the roof. *Nächste Abfahrt Richtung Hannover* it said on the placard above it. The clock's fingers were set at 7.45. The platform was crowded with workers, many of them carrying satchels or small attaché cases.

Presently they heard the locomotive coming, and it hissed and cranked and whushed up alongside the platform. There was a surge of movement as the people on the platform rushed towards the doors, running alongside the still moving train, anxious to get aboard and make sure of a seat in the already crowded carriages. Curses, shouts of anger, a babel of noise and protest mingled with the shrill hiss of escaping steam and the shout of the station guard, an elderly man who watched the milling mass of struggling people with a spectacular lack of interest. It happened these days at every station on the line, and it no longer even merited comment. Nobody would complain, anyway. Nobody dared. Crowded, uncomfortable, expensive, unreliable – the trains might be all of these things – but no one would complain. All that mattered was getting to work, hopefully on time, not too late at any rate. Being a few minutes late, if the train had been held up, was barely excusable. Absenteeism without a medical certificate was totally forbidden. So you had to be on your train in the morning, and ready for work at eight-thirty, or else.

'What a life, eh?' wheezed a fat man in a heavy woollen overcoat that smelled of mothballs. His wide-brimmed hat dripped moisture and his bulging belly was jammed up against Miller's chest, pinning the smaller man against another equally portly German in a leather jacket. Miller was having all he could do to breathe, so he just nodded.

'I've seen cattle better treated than this,' agreed Leather Jacket. 'It's scandalous.'

'They ought to put on extra carriages,' agreed a motherly-looking woman sitting on the seat directly under Moth Balls' elbow. She looked around defiantly as though daring anyone to disagree with her.

'It's the war,' Moth Balls said.

'The war, always the war,' the woman muttered.

'Tush,' said Leather Jacket. 'It said on the radio this morning the war will be over in another six months.'

'Really?' Chevalier said, feigning interest as Leather Jacket looked right at him. 'I missed it. What else did it say?'

'Ach, the usual,' Leather Jacket said. 'Bombers over England again. London, Coventry, Liverpool. They say our boys will be in Piccadilly next April, and home by summer.'

'Let's hope they bring some railway carriages with them,' snapped the woman, and there was a burst of laughter from the other passengers at her sally. Even the sour-faced man with the moth-ball smell managed a thin smile. The smile faded as the train jerked and began to slow down.

'Jesus God,' Moth Balls said. 'Can't they see there's no more room in here?'

They coasted into Poggenhagen, billows of steam

obscuring the faces of the waiting crowds on the platform. There was a repetition of the uproar they had witnessed at Neustadt, as the crowd of workers stormed the doorways, forcing themselves into the compartment, smiling to apologize for their having to use elbows and backs to make space, crushing those inside even closer together. They were already cramped like sardines, hands held against their bodies, trying wherever possible to keep their faces averted from that of the next person a foot away. The carriage smelled of sweat, and wet clothing, and coarse tobacco smoke. Chevalier had been pushed perhaps six or more feet away from Davidson and Whitehead, while Miller was still jammed between Moth Balls and Leather Jacket, trying to keep his chin above the level of their burly shoulders.

'God in Heaven!' shouted Leather Jacket. 'Stop pushing, there!'

'Get out and walk if you don't like it, Grandfather,' shouted a young fellow who was squirming to make a space upon which he could stand, further down the carriage. There was a scatter of laughter, and Davidson made a mental note of the essential good-naturedness of the heavy joking. Morale seemed high in Germany, in spite of conditions such as these.

'It'll ease off a little at Wunstorf,' Moth Balls assured him, nodding at everyone as though it was his personal responsibility to make them all feel a little better. 'Quite a few people get off at Wunstorf.'

'*Ja, ja,*' said a man who hadn't spoken so far, a thin, lantern-jawed fellow with a grubby white shirt and egg-spotted tie, whose off-white raincoat looked as if it had seen better days thirty years ago. 'And quite a few more get on, too.'

'Something really ought to be done,' another said.

'Go and complain at the Town Hall,' jeered a third voice, and there was a chorus of derisive whistles which faded as the motherly looking woman hissed at them for silence.

'Be still!' she said sharply, leaning across the elderly, bearded man in a black overcoat sitting next to her at the window seat, swabbing the condensation from the window with the sleeve of her coat. 'Something is happening out there!'

Everyone leaned over towards the windows, trying to see through the almost opaque film of steamy moisture coating them.

'What is it?' Davidson asked a man nearer to the window than himself.

'I can't see,' the man muttered. 'You, Madam, can you see? What is happening?'

Outside, they could seem men striding up and down the platform, and once or twice the grey of uniforms. The elderly bearded man sitting alongside the motherly woman pressed his face against the glass to peer out, then recoiled, as if the glass had suddenly become red-hot. His eyes were like those of a trapped animal, but he did not leave his seat.

'What is it?' Davidson repeated.

The woman looked at him with hard, incurious eyes.

'You don't know?' she said. 'They haven't made you late for work before?'

'Who?' he asked, feeling foolish.

'Why, the Gestapo,' she said primly. 'Who else?'

6

'Oh, is that who it is,' Davidson said, forcing a smile which he hoped would conceal the look of startled shock that the woman's words had brought involuntarily to his face. 'I couldn't see.'

Moving as unobtrusively as he could, he started to un-button the long overcoat he was wearing, the better to be able to reach the Walther P38 tucked into his waistband. Chevalier saw his movement and reached across, touching Davidson's arm. He shook his head impercep-tibly. 'Wait,' he mouthed.

As he spoke, four grey-caped *Schutzpolizei,* one of them a squat, perspiring sergeant, were thrusting their way into the compartment, their shiny patent-leather helmets bobbing above the heads of the passengers as they roughly cleared a path down the centre of the carriage. Into this space stepped a very tall, dark-haired man dressed in a military-style raincoat and a black slouch hat with a wide silvery band, the brim of which was pulled down all the way around. Had it not been for the sneering expression which pulled his thin-lipped mouth out of shape, he might almost have been hand-some. His shrewd dark eyes surveyed the crowded carriage and its passengers with undisguised contempt. He nodded to the perspiring *Schutzpolizei* sergeant, who bustled forward. 'Papers, papers!' he shouted. 'Show your papers immediately.'

The other policemen followed behind him, hands on the tops of their unbuttoned pistol holsters, snatching the identity cards from the extended hands and whirling with machine-like precision to show them to the apparently indifferent Gestapo man.

'Show your papers, hold them up!' shouted the sergeant, pushing his way between Davidson and Whitehead. 'Get back there, you!' he snapped at the former when Davidson set his weight on his heels and resisted the shove. Davidson stepped aside, his head hanging low in shame, and Whitehead breathed a sigh of relief. This was no time to shove back.

'What are they looking for?' he whispered urgently to Chevalier.

'God knows,' was the sibilant reply. 'Us, maybe.'

It was a distinct possibility. Perhaps the plane had been spotted after all. Perhaps some roving farmer had seen them and reported to the police. Perhaps their equipment, although well-concealed, had been found by schoolchildren playing in the woods. Perhaps the Manchester had been brought down, its crew only just interrogated. All these possibilities flashed through the minds of the waiting men as the languid Gestapo man drew nearer to them. All they could do was to fish out the identity papers that had been prepared for them and pray that Q section was as good as everyone said it was.

The *Schutzpolizei* snatched the papers out of their hands, thrust them beneath the Gestapo man's disdainful nose, waited. He shook his head, using the minimal movement, and the policeman handed them back to their owners without another word. Davidson could feel Chevalier's whole frame tensing for movement as the Gestapo man looked at the identity card, then into his face. Then he pushed past Chevalier, who almost fell, grabbing at the Gestapo man's shoulder.

'Oh, excuse me, sir,' he said. 'It was my fault, excuse me.'

The man seemed to be about to say something when one of the policemen thrust the identity card of the small, bearded man by the window beneath his gaze. The dark eyes narrowed, and the Gestapo man nodded. '*Raus!*' he snapped. 'Take him out!'

Two of the *Schutzpolizei* grabbed the old man by the arms, yanking him, unresisting, out of his seat and frogmarching him down the aisle now formed by the passengers, who shrank away from the trio as if they were contaminated. There was a rank smell of terror in the air and everyone's eyes were on the Gestapo man. If he was conscious of it, he gave no sign, but continued his leisurely inspection of the identity cards. The two policemen came hurrying back and took their places behind him as before.

'Another, *Herr Hauptmann!*' snapped the policeman further up the carriage, and the Gestapo man was beside him in two pantherish bounds. He glanced at the identity card and nodded, and the fat sergeant yanked a young boy of about eighteen to his feet. The boy's lower lip was trembling with terror, and his eyes implored those nearest to him to help. He might as well have been appealing to stone statues. Those sitting next to him, those standing around, averted their eyes, stared at the floor, each other, out of the windows.

'Get this whelp out of here!' snapped the tall man, and the two soldiers bundled the unfortunate youngster the length of the carriage, pushing him out of the door ahead of them. He sprawled painfully on the concrete platform, his face white and shocked, and was dragged to his feet by the two policemen, who shoved him over to where a group of perhaps a dozen people stood shivering in the cutting wind on the open platform. Davidson noticed that there were one or two women among them, and was about to lean forward to see more clearly when the fat sergeant turned around and yelled at the top of his voice 'All right, all right! Never mind what's going on outside. It's none of your concern.'

Eyes were hastily averted from the windows, and now the passengers all stared straight ahead, their faces as expressionless as window-mannequins.

'So!' the sergeant said, nodding. 'In order!' He turned and opened the connecting door to the next carriage for the Gestapo officer, who nodded and went through, followed by the other policemen. They could hear the fat sergeant's raised voice shouting 'Papers! Papers!' quite clearly because of the dead silence in the carriage. Then, slowly, the tension dissipated; the awful, tangible smell of animal terror seeped away and people began to talk very quietly, heads downcast.

'Well, what the devil was all that about?' Whitehead said to the man in the leather jacket. The man's head came up, fear and astonishment written on his face.

'*Gott in Himmel!*' he said in shocked tones. 'Keep your voice down!'

Moth Balls leaned over and tapped Whitehead on the shoulder.

'Listen, friend,' he said. 'If you haven't learned to keep your mouth shut when the Gestapo's around, you're not long for this world.'

'I know that,' Whitehead said, in pretended impatience. 'I just wondered . . . .'

'Take my advice,' Leather Jacket said. 'Don't.'

Whitehead frowned, and leaned to one side so that he could see out of the patch that the old man had swabbed clear on the window. The little group of men and women was being herded towards the station exit by a squad of soldiers, greatcoats swinging as they prodded their prisoners along with the barrels of their rifles. The people walked with heads down, like stunned animals, cowed and unprotesting. There was no expression on the faces of the soldiers. They looked like soldiers anywhere, doing a boring, thankless, underpaid job, their expression that of cowherds driving cattle in for milking.

After about another ten minutes, the train whistle shrieked, a long blast followed by two short ones. Then the carriage jerked as the engine shunner-shunner-shunnered into motion with a clattering clank of couplings. In a moment they were picking up speed, the driver anxious to make up time so that he could have his coffee before he turned round and came back in time to pick up the clerical workers. Out of the windows on the left hand side, Chevalier could see the busy road between Wunstorf and Gümmer, until a stretch of pine forest obscured it from view. The roar of the train deepened as they passed beneath the concrete arches of the autobahn.

'Boy,' Miller said, sidling around Leather Jacket until he was close enough to whisper without being overheard. The others huddled nearer.

'What do you think it was all about, Skipper?'

'God knows,' Chevalier replied softly. 'The Gestapo doesn't have to explain to anyone.'

'One thing,' Davidson said, thoughtfully. The others

looked at him. 'I'd say all those people had something in common.'

Whitehead nodded. 'I thought the same thing. Jewish, you mean?'

Davidson said nothing, just looked his question.

'So why are the Gestapo rounding up Jewish people?' Miller asked.

'That's a good question,' Chevalier said.

'Could it have anything to do with us? Whitehead asked.

'That's another,' Chevalier replied.

After that they were silent for a long time. They did not speak again until the train pulled with a squeal of brakes and a flourish of escaping steam into the Hauptbahnhof at Seelze. The time on the station clock was 8.43.

7

'This is where we split up,' Chevalier said.

They were standing on the corner of the Bahnhofstrasse, across the street from the railway station, outside
a *Konditorei* which had a ragged queue of housewives
waiting to be served. The smell of fresh pastries wafted
out to them each time the door opened, bell tinkling.

Once off the train they had moved swiftly. The haversacks had been left at the left luggage office, but not the
long slim case now firmly clutched in Davidson's meaty
fist. Chevalier had a slim leather briefcase, and Miller a
flat, leather, zippered folder which contained elec-
trician's tools. Their cover identities had been carefully
worked out long before they had left England. Davidson
and Whitehead carried papers identifying them as sur-
veyors for the *Niedersachsischen Landesvermessung,* the
local Governmental mapmaking authority; and in the
long slim case was a lightweight folding tripod and a
theodolite, together with a folding, wooden, standing
measure and a pair of small but very powerful Zeiss
binoculars. It was the fervent hope of both men that
anyone who stopped to question them would know even
less about geodetic surveying than they did.

Miller's papers showed him to be an inspector of
overhead cables for the State Electricity Authority, while
Chevalier's showed him to be an authorised representative of the *Bund deutscher Mädchen* the female equiva-

lent of the Hitler Youth. His battered briefcase was full of pamphlets and other literature about the movement. These would give him some excuse for being on the streets during the rigidly-enforced working hours, and the hobble he was now affecting would explain to any but a serious inquirer why he was not doing an able-bodied man's work. Miller's cover would enable him to move freely around the marshalling yards, railway tracks, and electrical sub-stations on both sides of the Hauptbahnhof, some of which were directly opposite the factory complex half a mile down the road to the west, and it was the job of Davidson and Whitehead to vet the factory area under the guise of surveying to establish means of entry and optimum locations for the explosives now lodged in the station left luggage office.

'You all know what to do,' Chevalier said. 'Any questions?'

'Rendezvous,' Davidson said softly.

'I repeat,' Chevalier said, an edge of testiness touching his tone. 'On the corner of the Havelsestrasse, one block up the Bahnhofstrasse from here.'

'Kreisler's,' Miller said.

'You can't miss it,' Chevalier said, unsmilingly. 'It's right next door to Gestapo headquarters.'

'Thanks,' Whitehead said, with a not-so-mock shudder.

'Eleven-thirty earliest, eleven forty-five latest,' Chevalier said. 'Rules as before.'

They nodded, taking his meaning. If any of them was captured or taken in for interrogation, then the others aborted the mission and did the best they could to get away.

'*Auf Wiedersehen,*' Davidson said, extending his hand. Chevalier shook it, and Davidson turned away, Whitehead loping alongside him as they headed up the Bahnhofstrasse.

'Where are we going?' Whitehead said as they strode through the busy street, crossing the Havelsestrasse and noting that Kreisler's was full of German soldiers.

'Get the layout of the place fixed in our heads,' Davidson explained briefly. 'Bahnhofstrasse runs north and south. To the right, Havelsestrasse. To the left, opposite, Schulstrasse. Far end of Schulstrasse, running north, parallel to Bahnhofstrasse, Goethestrasse. From Goethestrasse to Bahnhofstrasse, on our left but about a quarter of a mile north, Wiesenweg. Past Wiesenweg, Banhofstrasse makes an S-bend, crosses bridge over river Leine. Got it?'

'Got it,' Whitehead said, as they walked up the Bahnhofstrasse, dodging prams pushed by dumpy housewives who giggled when passing soldiers clicked their tongues and bowed, smiling at them, or chucked their babies under the chin.

'Right,' Davidson said. 'Off Goethestrasse is a U-shaped road with no name. It enters and leads out of the main administration building at the plant. There's a seven foot wire fence, probably electrified.'

'Right again,' Whitehead said. 'What's all this got to do with . . . .'

'Wait,' Davidson said, nodding cordially at two SS officers who were passing. 'Between the fence and the Goethestrasse, up at the north end where it joins the Wiesenweg, there's a patch of waste land. At least I hope it's still there. That's where we're going now.'

'Does it lead down to the river bank?'

'Ten out of ten,' Davidson said. 'How did you guess ?'

'Just plain brilliance, I expect,' Whitehead suggested as Davidson came to a stop at the corner of a street.

'On the right, Alte Dorfstrasse,' Davidson said. 'Leads to the main road on the eastern end of the Hauptbahnhof and forms the eastern edge of the village.'

'Thank you, ladies and gentlemen,' Whitehead said. 'The next tour begins promptly at 9.45. No dogs, no babies, no little old ladies in wheelchairs.'

'Come on,' Davidson said with a grin. He was beginning to like this big, bald-headed man who was less like a scientist than any scientist Captain George Stuart Davidson had ever encountered.

Miller, meanwhile, was having a cup of coffee. He had tested the door of a tar-paper roofed hut on the northern edge of the marshalling yards and almost fallen inside, where he startled a roughly-dressed gang of men who looked up in alarm at his intrusion, then welcomed him in to share their mid-morning snack. They were a platelaying gang, they told him, pressing cold sausage and dark, crusty bread on him. He had his work cut out not to wolf the food, so hungry was he. But he waved away the offer of another slice.

'Not for me,' he said. 'Too much work to do.'

'Haven't we all,' the foreman laughed. He was a thickset man with a strong Saxony accent, who said he came from Stöcken. 'There's never any end to the work.'

'Could be worse,' said another. 'We could be in the army.'

'God forbid,' a third man said fervently. They laughed, pouring more coffee for Miller from the blackened tin kettle on the cast-iron stove that filled the wooden hut with friendly, muggy warmth.

'You fellows do yourselves all right,' he told them. 'Very nice.' He waved a hand at the hut.

'You wouldn't say that if you had to work the hours we do,' the foreman said. 'I'd swap you any day, working office hours like you do.'

'You wouldn't say that,' Miller grinned, mimicking the foreman's words, 'if you had to shin up an electricity pylon in the middle of some damned snowstorm.'

'True enough,' the thin-faced man on his right muttered. 'Everyone to his own trade, I say. Fancy a cigarette ?'

'Don't mind if I do,' Miller said, as the thin-faced man pulled a flat tin out his pocket. He opened it and offered it to Miller, who picked out a cigarette. He froze : the pale blue lettering clearly read *Player's Medium Navy Cut*. saying nothing, he leaned forward as the thin-faced man struck a wooden match, his eyes moving across the other faces around him. No one seemed to have noticed anything. Miller felt the sweat in the palm of his hand and drew greedily on the cigarette.

'You like English cigarettes ?' the foreman said.

'Eh ?' Miller said, startled. 'What ?'

'Those,' the thin-faced one said. 'What you're smoking.'

Miller managed to look surprised, and took the cigarette from his mouth. 'I thought it tasted different,' he said. 'Where in the name of heaven do you get English cigarettes.'

The foreman smiled, and laid a gloved finger alongside his nose, winking as he did so.

'You work on the railway long enough,' he said. 'You know where to get everything. They captured millions of them after our boys kicked the British out of France. If you know who to ask . . . .'

He grinned again.

'Who wants more coffee?' one of the others asked, getting up off his chair and picking up the blackened kettle in a gloved hand. He held it up in the air, steam wisping from its spout, a query implicit in his raised brows. Miller nodded and held out his cup.

'Warm you up, that will,' the man said.

'I can do with it,' Miller told him. 'Walking as much as I do.'

'Don't tell us,' the thin-faced man said. 'You get a freeze, maybe half a centimetre of ice on the rails, they'll have us out at three in the morning to clear it. They don't care if the damned tracks freeze as fast as you thaw them. Specially over at that blasted place over on the far side of town.'

'Big place, that,' Miller said idly. 'They must use a lot of power.'

'Wouldn't be surprised,' the foreman agreed. 'They've got top priority on everything else around here, that lot. Take us, we have to keep their feeder lines in top condition, all the year round and to the devil with the weather.'

'That's what I said,' the thin-faced man put in. 'Three in the morning, they don't care.'

'Well,' Miller said, putting his cup down on the lino-covered table top. 'Got to get moving. I've to check this whole section today.'

'Good luck to you, mate,' the thin faced man said. 'Drop in again if you feel like a hot drink.'

'And if you want anything else,' the foreman said, stressing the last word. 'Off the back of the truck, if you know what I mean. Schnapps, maybe. Or some good *Speck*. Or cigarettes, let us know. We might be able to help.' He grinned and winked, giving Miller a light nudge.

'Well,' Miller said. 'Thanks. If I do, I'll let you know. What's the best time to find you here?'

'Oh, there's always some of the gang around, day or night,' the foreman said. 'Just tell whoever you see you want to leave a message for Schultz. Everyone knows me.'

'Thanks,' Miller said. 'I may look in again.'

'Any time,' the foreman said. 'Swing shifts, we work. *Auf Wiedersehen.*'

'*Wiedersehen*,' Miller said, and went out into the siding, looking out across the maze of shining tracks. They glinted, picking up a faint hint of the morning sun trying to break through. His face looked thoughtful. It wasn't going to be all that easy to move around here if there were always workmen about. Still, it remained to be seen whether they'd need to. He grinned to himself: Germany wasn't any different to anywhere else. London had its spivs, and here they weren't too particular about flogging off anything they could get hold of: captured cigarettes or food that had been found before it was lost. Everybody wanted a few quid extra if they could get hold of it without being noticed. He looked along the lines, gauging the distance to the platforms of the station. About four hundred yards.

I don't know why the hell I'm doing all this, he told himself with a shrug. But he did it anyway, estimating how far the sound would carry, and from which angles men moving in the station or alongside the tracks might be seen by men working the graveyard shift and using the platelayers hut. Sound would carry a long way on a cold winter's night : it was as well to know the gangs might be there.

He struck out now back alongside the right of way, traversing the length of the station platform and getting the layout of it firmly imprinted on his brain. Using the ramp on the far side, he descended to the tracks again and crossed the wide iron bridge which carried them across the Bahnhofstrasse. He headed west, leaving the station behind as he came towards the feeder junction where wagons were shunted in and out of the factory complex. He looked at the maze of tracks and points and signals and shook his head ruefully. Then he continued on his way, a tuneless whistle that might have been 'The Blue Danube' on his lips. Just ten minutes later he was busily screwing off the inspection cover on the junction box of a telephone transformer which stood no more than a hundred yards from the main entrance to the Reidel and de Hahn administration building on the far side of the Wunstorferstrasse.

Chevalier had worked his way up one side of the Alte Dorfstrasse and down the other, knocking at the doors of the neat villas for more than an hour, trotting out the memorized spiel to perhaps two dozen housewives, whose reactions had ranged from a quickly-slammed door, through apathy (barely polite), all the way to violent argument. One – a plump Bavarian blonde with shortsighted blue eyes, still in a dressing gown which was open wide enough to show her ample breasts – had quite definitely had other things on her mind when she invited him inside to explain his proposition more fully. For the

69

first time, Chevalier began to see why the British adored their music-hall comedians. (*Sorry, lidy, but I 'aven't got the time. Echyah. I thankyow!* Exit, to trombone music.) Here and there, he had even exchanged half-baked theological philosophies with them; enough, he hoped, to convince anyone who might be watching him that he was what his papers said he was.

Now he crossed the Havelsestrasse where it joined the Alte Dorfstrasse, walking south towards the Hauptbahnhof. There was only one house on this side of the street, a big white two-storey house with green shutters and bare tendrils of ivy streaking the walls at one side. It was surrounded by a high wall, and there was an imposing gateway at which stood a sentry-box manned by a very bored-looking soldier. In the driveway Chevalier could see a parked Mercedes saloon, painted the dull military green, a swastika pennant on the left-hand wing. He took a deep breath and walked towards the gate. The sentry took a look at Chevalier's genteel-shabby clothes and half-heartedly ported the rifle.

'Hold on, there!' he snapped as Chevalier came level. Chevalier raised his eyebrows.

'Excuse me,' he said. 'Is this a military establishment?'

'Are you a stranger here?' the guard asked.

'I'm from Hanover,' Chevalier said. 'Who lives here?'

'None of your concern,' the guard said. 'Now, off with you. I haven't got time to stand here gossiping.'

'Perhaps you would like to read . . . ,' Chevalier began, fumbling his case open and bringing out a clutch of the BdM. pamphlets. The guard held up a free hand, an uneasy smile on his face.

'Not me,' he said. 'I don't go in for any of that stuff.'

'Ah, but that's the whole point,' Chevalier insisted. 'You see . . . .'

'Listen, be on your way, will you?' the guard hissed. 'There's someone coming!'

He looked nervously up towards the house, and Chevalier saw that two men were coming out, a German officer and a tall, grey-haired man in a dark overcoat. He got an impression of the face – beak-nosed, heavy horn-rimmed glasses, ruddy complexion – as the two men got into the Mercedes. The driver, who must have been sitting in the vehicle waiting, gunned the engine and turned the car around, and Chevalier eased back as the sentry snapped to attention. The car slowed down as it came out of the gateway, and he was able to see the two men inside quite clearly now. The officer wore the insignia of a *Sturmbannführer* SS – rank roughly equivalent to Chevalier's own – and the silver skull-and-crossbones cap badge meant he belonged to the Third Panzer Division, the *Totenkopf,* whose leader was Heinrich Himmler himself. The face Chevalier glimpsed was pudgy, and the man had that heavy shadow of stubble beneath the skin which the French call *barbe-bleu.* Rimless glasses, and a weak, almost sensuous mouth, completed the quick impression he gathered as the driver moved smoothly out into the Dorfstrasse and then turned right along the main road past the station.

'Who was that?' he asked the guard.

'That,' said the sentry heavily, 'that was *Sturmbannführer* Klaus Flügge, that's who that was.'

'And who's he, may I ask?'

The sentry looked heavily at Chevalier, to see if there was any trace of mockery on his face. Seeing none, he nodded forgivingly.

'You being a stranger here wouldn't know, I suppose,' he said. 'He's the head of the military in this region.'

'Does he live here?'

'That he does, and so does the Doctor.'

'That was the grey-haired man.'

'Dr Karl Heineman,' the sentry said. 'One of the Reich's most famous scientists.'

'He lives *here*?'

He accented the words just right, for the guard smiled.

'Heard of *him,* have you? Yes he lives here. The house is his. But we keep an eye on him.'

'That's a big responsibility, guarding so important a man,' Chevalier said, admiringly. 'All on your own.'

'Oh, there's half a . . . see here, I can't spend the day chattering to you. Now be off. There's no chance of your going up to the house, so you're just wasting your time.'

'Yes, yes, to be sure,' Chevalier said hastily. 'Thank you, Sergeant, thank you very much. Until I see you again.'

'See you,' the soldier said, primping pompously at the fool's assumption that he was a sergeant. Chevalier limped off up the street, satisfied with what he had found out. He turned left at the Havelsestrasse, walking along on the right hand side past the church with its unkempt cemetery, crossing the Kirchstrasse and walking up the block until he came to a shop with the sign BÄCKEREI hanging at right angles over the door. On the window was painted the legend BÄCKEREI RENNER GEG. 1922. He pushed open the door and went in. There were two or three housewives waiting to be served and he stood patiently, waiting his turn. There were two women behind the counter. One was quite obviously the mother of the other, for both had the same heart-shaped features, the same mobile, full lips, and both the same beautiful chestnut hair. Frau Renner was, however, dumpy and motherly, her arms and bosom ample, while her daughter was slender, her movements indicating that beneath the shapeless smock she wore was the body of a beautiful woman.

'Good morning, sir,' she said, smiling as Chevalier moved up to the counter.

'Good morning, miss,' he said. 'I wonder . . . have you any yeast?'

Her eyes widened, and for a moment she stood stock still. Then, in the space of another heartbeat, she had complete control of herself and was smiling again. 'I'm not sure,' she said. 'Mother, is there any yeast?'

'Look in the back room, *Liebchen,*' Frau Renner said.

'Can you wait a moment?' the girl asked Chevalier.

'I can wait as long as you wish,' Chevalier told her, completing the recognition code. She nodded and went into the back room, emerging shortly empty-handed.

'Alas,' she said, spreading her hands. 'We have none left.'

'Ach, shame,' Chevalier said, looking upset. 'I have to have some by one o'clock.' He looked at the girl levelly.'Can you suggest anything? I'm a stranger here.'

'Perhaps you can get some at Hinkel's,' she replied. 'Here, I'll write down the address for you.'

She scribbled something on a paper bag, handing it to Chevalier.

'I thank you very much,' he said. '*Auf wiedersehen, Fräulein.*'

'*Auf wiedersehen,*' Jutta Renner replied, her wide green eyes touched faintly with apprehension. Then, as

73

Chevalier left the shop, she gave a shake to herself, as if mentally adjusting her balance, and turned smiling to the next customer with a cheerful greeting.

Chevalier walked back along the street to the corner of the Kirchstrasse, where he stopped and unfolded the paper bag. REAR BAKERY ONE OKAY, he translated as he read, and nodded, putting the paper bag into his coat pocket. He looked up as the church clock chimed the hour. Eleven o'clock. Chevalier nodded, satisfied. He was right on schedule.

Davidson and Whitehead walked boldly along the Wiesenweg, the former with the tripod over his shoulder, the latter carrying the leather case. Halfway along, they found a footpath no wider than a sheeptrack leading off to the right, downhill into a timbered bottom where the river Leine ran, purling in a long curve north-west towards the Mittellandkanal. They looked around. Apart from a housewife shaking out a rug in her garden, there was nobody in sight. They went quickly down the footpath until they reached the screen of willow and proliferating shrubbery along the river bank. There was another footpath following the edge of the river. Here and there, about ten yards apart, there were places where the bushes had been pushed back and the grass was flattened and dried.

'Lover's lane ?' Davidson hazarded.

'Be as well to remember that if we have to come down here at night,' Whitehead said. 'Probably more of the glorious Wehrmacht down here than in the barracks.'

They walked along the pathway until it petered out in a screen of scrubby trees through which they could see the metallic glint of the fence surrounding the factory

74

complex. They pushed on to the end of the copse, and set up the theodolite looking out across the river towards the distant buildings of Havelse. Whitehead clamped the binoculars on to the neat clip which had been fixed to the revolving turret, and focussed them, ignoring the telescopic sight on the theodolite, whose range would not be sufficient for what he needed. While he did this, Davidson clambered down towards the river's edge, extending the huge scale rule. Feeling vaguely foolish, since nobody was watching them – as far as he could tell – Whitehead waved his arm for Davidson to move left. And then left again. And then left again, until he was standing with his back towards the angle of the high fence around the complex. Once more Whitehead waved his arm, and then he bent to the binoculars. Through them he could clearly see the layer of six-inch effluent pipes emerging from the *Kläranlage,* the cleaning plant, to the right of which, easily identifiable by the yellow plates with their ACHTUNG ! warning signs showing lightning flashes, was the smaller effluent generator plant. Whitehead stifled a curse. The laboratory lay directly behind the huge effluent plant. They would have to move around further to the west before he could see it clearly. He waved Davidson in and, folding the eight-foot measure, the Scot came over to where Whitehead stood.

'What's up, Doc ?' he grinned.

Whitehead told him, and Davidson's humour evaporated.

'That river's got ice on it,' he pointed out.

'As long as it hasn't got alligators,' Whitehead said, moving off with the tripod over his shoulder. As Davidson fell in step he said, 'Did you take a look at the fence ?'

'That I did,' was the grim reply. 'It would be a mistake to touch it.'

They scrambled now down the sleek, sloping side of the swirling stream, shoes sticking in sucking slime. Directly ahead, the huge six-inch drains projected from the concrete ramp which had been placed at the river's edge behind the factory. A trickle of liquid was coming from them, dribbling sibilantly into the river.

'Effluent,' Whitehead explained.

'You too,' Davidson replied.

'Any chemical plant needs a waste outlet,' Whitehead explained patiently, ignoring Davidson's humour – if that was the word for it. 'Here, they're taking pains to clean the waste before releasing it into the river, for obvious reasons.'

'Poisons the fish, you mean ?'

'Rather more than that,' Whitehead said. 'If my memory is correct, the Leine is one of the major sources of water for Hanover. There's a big series of reservoirs and filtering plants between here and the city, with the central one at Ricklingen. You can imagine what might happen if any of friend Heineman's experimental stuff was dumped into the water without being very thoroughly screened, can't you ?'

'It's a tempting thought,' Davidson admitted. 'I suppose we . . . ?'

'You know we couldn't,' Whitehead said.

'I suppose you're right,' sighed Davidson. Now they moved carefully along the slimy edge of the river, which was littered with waterlogged sticks, slime-encrusted bottles, rusted cans. Ready to hunt cover at the first sign of any guard, they were almost clear of the effluent pipes when Whitehead felt the ground tremor, and heard a far-off rumbling like a train entering a tunnel.

'Get out of here!' he shouted at Davidson, pushing the Scot hard as he did. Davidson's feet slithered and for a horrible moment he fought to keep his balance, even as from the mouth of the exit pipes there came a growling, rushing sound, somewhere between a gargantuan belch and a gigantic gurgle, followed by the most awful, overpowering stench. Whitehead, already moving flat out, caught at Davidson as he drew level with the reeling Scot, dragging him forward and down away from the pipes, scrabbling, lurching, falling several times into the shallow fringes of the river for ten, fifteen, twenty feet as the rumbling in the pipes became an immense roar and, without warning, an enormous series of spouts of liquid burst from the pipes. Outwards they arched, a dozen feet or more, stinking, vile, mud-coloured, churning the surface of the previously-limpid Leine to a brown and ugly foam from which steam rose, and upon which evil-smelling bubbles formed and burst. Serried, roiling, riverbed mud squirmed almost like some huge snake as the cascade roared on and on and on; five, seven, ten, almost twelve minutes. Then, as abruptly as it had begun, the roar ceased, the arch of effluent faltered, dropped, broke, trickled and stopped.

'Well,' Davidson said, getting slowly to his feet. 'That won't do the fishes much good.' He turned to Whitehead with a guarded smile. 'Doc,' he said. 'I don't know whether I ought to give you a whack for pushing me or shake your hand for grabbing me – but . . . .'

'Forget it,' Whitehead told him. 'We're not finished here yet.'

'Onward Christian Soldiers,' Davidson muttered as

Whitehead pushed on along the river bank, away from the stink of the effluent pipes, to a point on the edge of the river where trees grew fringing the bank, their branches dipping here and there into the water, quite clear here upstream, and moving gently towards the muddy mess behind them. Lying against the sloping bank, feet towards the water beneath the trees, they could see quite clearly now into the open space at the rear of the complex.

They were facing due south, give or take a point of the compass. To the right of where they lay were two big sheds, oblong in shape, set at right angles to each other. Railway tracks ran into each on the side furthest away from the hidden watcher, and on this side lorries were backed in to a concrete ramp for loading. Whitehead let the binoculars follow the pipes entering the effluent plant until he saw where they entered the laboratory. They would slope down into a basement, he imagined. Now he gave his full attention to the laboratory itself. A big one-storey structure at the rear, while at the southern end there was a block built on to make it two storeys high. To connect, presumably, with the general admin. block, he guessed. He was about to hand the binoculars to Davidson, when a movement caught his eye.

'Get down!' he hissed.

They flattened their faces into the long grass, peering upwards as they saw the guard coming along the perimeter fence, Schmeisser canted casually across his forearm, while straining at the short leash in his other hand was a vicious-looking black dog.

'Doberman Pinscher,' whispered Davidson, as the animal gave a thin whine and tugged the guard toward the fence, pulling hard on the leash and barking, it seemed to the two hidden men, directly at them.

'What's wrong, Fritzi?' the soldier said, unslinging the Schmeisser. He stood with the machine-pistol at port, eyes sweeping right and left across the arc of his vision.

'There's nothing there, dog,' he said impatiently.

The dog continued to bark, and the man shook the leash impatiently, dragging the reluctant animal around, slinging his gun across his shoulder in disgust.

'Come on, you thickhead,' he snapped. 'I've got no time to chase rabbits.'

He dragged the Doberman away and, after a few moments, the dog gave up the unequal struggle and trotted docilely at the soldier's heels. Davidson drew what seemed like his first full breath in a week.

'Whew,' he said. 'I wonder how many of those there are?'

'Pray God we never have to find out,' Whitehead said piously. 'Come on, your turn with the glasses.'

Davidson took the binoculars and scanned the area, noting and estimating mentally the thickness and solidity of the walls, and in particular the window frames of the buildings he could see. He noted that, to the rear of the general administration building, there was a parking area in which he could see both civilian and military vehicles standing. He asked Whitehead a question.

'German method,' Whitehead guessed. 'Each building will have a block number. Let me take a look.'

He focussed the glasses on the point that Davidson had indicated and made out the big, sansserif figure 5 painted on the corner of the loading shed to their right. Stowing the glasses away, he nodded. 'The loading shed is block five,' he said. 'We can make a rough guess at the others : the main admin. building will be Block 1, the general admin. Block 2, Labs Block 3. And so on.'

Davidson nodded. 'Well?' he said. 'Have we seen everything?'

'I guess so,' Whitehead replied. 'Let's get back to dry land. I want to take a look around the front.'

The Scot glanced quickly at his watch.

'Ten fifty-three,' he said. 'We'll have to look smart.'

'Right,' Whitehead agreed. 'So don't just sit there.'

8

'Let's hear it,' Chevalier said.

They were sitting at a corner table in Kreisler's, welcome cups of warm, if weak, coffee on the check tablecloth in front of them. It was only a small place, perhaps a dozen tables altogether; two in the lace-curtained window looking out on to the Bahnhofstrasse, and then two rows in line with them, one row up against the big floor-to-ceiling windows looking out into the Havelsestrasse, the other down the middle of the room. Beyond them was a long counter on which were ranged pastries and fruit tarts. At the end of this counter, near the door, was the cash desk, presided over by Frau Kreisler, a sharp-faced woman with a prune-like mouth, who surveyed each customer that entered as if he were a convicted thief. Apart from four women at a table looking out over the Bahnhofstrasse, who were so deep in their *Kaffeeklatsch* as to be oblivious of anyone in the place, the only other customers were two soldiers and an elderly man wearing the grey uniform of a railwayman.

'Factory zone,' Davidson said, his voice pitched low so that it would not travel across the room. 'Two entrances, two exits, all guarded. Passes checked going in and coming out. The fence is electrified – the signs say 2000 volts and I believe them.'

'Dog patrols,' Whitehead added, 'every ten minutes.'

'Assuming entry – for the moment,' Chevalier said.

'Very vulnerable,' Davidson said with certainty in his voice. 'Very vulnerable indeed.'

'Dusty?'

'Marshallin' yards taken care of,' Miller said. 'Shift workers, but all at the eastern end. Electrical's a doddle. I can put that line out of action in 'alf a minute.'

'How about the complex?'

'More difficult, that,' Miller replied. 'Got their own generators, so they can keep goin' even if the main supplies are knocked out.'

'Again, assuming entry.'

'No problem. There's enough overhead wires in that place to stretch from here to London.'

'Good,' Chevalier said.

'How about you?' Davidson asked. 'Any joy?'

'Some,' Chevalier said. 'The Heineman house has six guards – plain soldiers, not SS – but it would be hard to take quietly. The local military commander also lives there.'

'So we'd have to take him at the factory?'

'Looks like it,' Chevalier said. 'Something else.'

They looked at him expectantly.

'I've made contact with our agent here. She's the daughter of the people who own the bakery across the street – no, don't look now. Pretty girl,' he mused. 'She'll provide us with a safe place to lie low until we make our move.'

'Which will be when?'

'Five p.m.,' Chevalier said. 'It gets dark at about four-thirty, so we'll be able to make the maximum use of darkness and the resulting confusion.'

'What's the plan?' Whitehead asked.

'Not here,' Chevalier said, looking around warily.

Frau Kreisler was glaring at them from the cash desk. It was getting close to the lunch hour and she didn't want her tables occupied by people who only bought coffee. 'We leave one by one, Miller first. Go out of here and turn into the Havelsestrasse. Turn left at the Kirchstrasse. There's a narrow alley running behind the shops, where they make deliveries. The bakery has a loading ramp with a set of stairs at the side, leading to a door. It's marked BÄCKEREI RENNER. PRIVAT. Go in and wait there for the rest of us. Whitehead, you'll follow, then you, Davidson. I'll pay the bill here and join you. Got it?'

They all nodded, and Dusty Miller got up, pushing back his chair and nodding goodbye to Frau Kreisler, who sniffed at him. After a moment or two, Whitehead got up, shook hands with the other two, and went out. Davidson and Chevalier waited for a few more minutes, pretending to empty their already empty cups, and then, while Chevalier paid the bill, Davidson went out of the café and turned right into the Havelsestrasse, walking confidently, head high. He was just turning into the Kirchstrasse as Chevalier crossed the street diagonally, in front of the Gestapo headquarters with its drooping swastika flag. Not hurrying, Chevalier turned into the street opposite the church, and then sharp left again into the alley, confident no one had noticed him. He walked rapidly along the alley, up the stairs alongside the ramp, and pushed open the door leading into the gloomy room at the rear of the bakery.

'Look . . . !'

He heard the strangled shout as Miller tried to warn him, and then saw a sudden movement as a German soldier slammed the little man to the ground with the butt of his rifle. Miller went down, writhing and groaning, and Chevalier backed against the door through which he had just entered, taking in the whole scene before him.

Standing with their hands on their heads, their faces the very picture of astonished dejection, stood Whitehead and Davidson. Behind them were ranged four tough-looking Waffen SS, rifles trained on their prisoners. In a chair, bound and gagged, her eyes rolling in helpless appeal, sat Jutta Renner, while behind the chair, leaning almost languidly against it, was a very tall, powerfully built man, in a trench-coat that might have been the twin of the one worn by the Gestapo man who had inspected their papers on the train. Unlike him, though, this man was not handsome. His flat-planed face was ugly, as marked as that of a professional boxer, the wide-bridged nose plainly showing that it had been broken at least twice, the skin around the mouth scarred and puckered. The deep-set eyes were shrewd and burningly intelligent, however, and he surveyed Chevalier with an almost amused detachment.

'Welcome to our little gathering, Major Chevalier,' he said, his voice soft and deep. 'Our little gathering of saboteurs and spies.'

'Sir,' Whitehead began plaintively. 'Herr Hauptmann, there has been a terrible mistake . . . .'

'Indeed,' the tall man said. 'And you have made it, Doctor Whitehead.'

Whitehead's eyes widened but he said nothing, watching as the tall man put his hand into an inside pocket and brought out a flat leather wallet which he flipped open, identifying himself.

'*Hauptsturmführer* Bernhard Geis, *Geheime Staats*

Polizei!' he snapped. 'In charge of Gestapo investigation, *Landkreis Hanover*.'

'Gestapo!' Davidson breathed.

'Yes, Captain Davidson,' Geis replied. 'Gestapo. We are not such fools as your deluded Special Operations Executive seems to think!'

'There's no answer to that,' Davidson said brightly. Without warning Geis's gloved hand lashed out, backhanding Davidson across the mouth and sending him reeling back against the wall, blood trickling from a split lip.

'You would do well to guard your tongue when you speak to me, Captain!' the Gestapo man snapped. 'This is not some stupid British film where you may show how brave you are. You are spies, and will be treated accordingly!'

He surveyed them all with an almost gentle smile that made his broken face seem quite pleasant, but there was nothing pleasant about the look in his eyes. It boded no good for someone.

'And little Warrant-Officer Miller,' he said softly. 'Help him up, Baumann, help him up. After all, he's almost as valuable a catch as these other . . . gentlemen. Warrant Officer Miller knows as much as there is to know about the quantity, quality, and disposition of Britain's telecommunications network, as indeed, he should. He has been working on them off and on since 1937, haven't you, Miller?'

'Go to hell!' spat Miller, shaking off the helping hand of the German sergeant who had earlier knocked him down.

'Hell is a purely relative place,' the Gestapo man said, silkily. 'As all of you will find if you do not . . .

co-operate. You, for instance, Doctor Whitehead. You seem to be anxious to meet our Dr Heineman. Well, you shall. He will be most interested to hear all about your work at Porton Down.'

'I'd sooner be shot,' Whitehead spat.

'Oh, don't worry, Doctor, you will be. But not before you have shared all your little secrets with us. Or Captain Davidson, here. We're so looking forward to hearing about your duties as Training Commander for MO9, Captain. We want to learn all the little tricks you have been teaching your so-called secret assault division, the Commandos.'

'I wouldn't want you to hang by the toes until you do,' Davidson said, sticking out his chin in a defiant gesture.

'Ah, such brave, foolhardy chatter,' Geis said. Then his expression and his voice hardened abruptly. 'But enough! You are saboteurs, spies! I would be quite within my rights to shoot you all like the dogs that you are! However,' his voice grew gentle again, and he turned to face Chevalier. 'I am being remiss in my duties. I have not welcomed your leader. Major.' Geis bowed slightly, clicking his heels.

'Who told you?' Miller shouted, unable to contain himself any longer. 'Who told you? Who was it? The girl?'

'Warrant Officer, if you do not control yourself I will have you ... silenced,' Geis said angrily. 'However, I will answer your question. No, it was not Fräulein Renner who betrayed you. If anything, she is a more valuable catch than the rest of you put together. Fräulein Renner, has of course, been working inside the Reich, privy to secrets which – unfortunately – she should never have learned. And, alas . . . .' He smilingly chucked the girl under the chin, the gesture almost a caress. 'She will have to pay the sad penalty for possessing that knowledge.'

'You swine!' Whitehead snapped. 'You couldn't have caught us without inside information! There weren't more than a dozen people in on this operation.'

'More than that, I think,' Geis said, ignoring Whitehead's anger. 'But you're right, of course. We did have inside information. About your plans, your identities, the people who sent you, and every move you made! From our top spy in England.'

'Me,' Chevalier said.

9

'You!' shouted Davidson. '*You?*' He made as if to move forward at Chevalier but, before he could get started, one of the German guards jammed his Schmeisser into his ribs with a growl of warning.

'Do not be foolish, Captain,' Geis smiled. 'We don't want to have to kill you . . . yet.'

'You bastard!' Davidson hissed. Chevalier ignored him.

'Allow me to introduce myself,' he said. 'Paul Ritter, *Oberstgruppenführer, Abwehr* – the espionage, counter-espionage and sabotage service of the High Command of the Third Reich!' He allowed himself a smile at the thunderstruck expressions upon the faces of the four prisoners, then turned to Geis, his face growing stern. 'I was beginning to think I might have to go through with the damned raid,' he said. 'Your people have not been particularly efficient, Geis.'

The Gestapo man's shoulders straightened, and the watchers thought they could detect anger deep in the hooded eyes.

'If you wish to take command here as senior officer, *Herr Oberst,* I . . . .'

Chevalier waved the suggestion aside. 'No need of that,' he said. 'Simply tell me what happens now. I must get to Headquarters and make my report. I have much valuable information to transmit to Berlin as soon as possible.'

'Understood, *Herr Oberst,*' Geis replied. 'Under normal circumstances prisoners like these would be taken under guard and put in the cells at Gestapo headquarters, across the street. From there, almost certainly, they would be taken under heavy guard to the maximum security prison at Schloss Ricklingen, and given the choice of either telling us everything they know about their respective occupations and duties, and thenceforward collaborating with the Reich, or shot.'

'I see,' Chevalier said, nodding. An afterthought occurred to him and his brow wrinkled as he spoke. 'Under normal circumstances?'

'Yes,' Geis nodded. 'You see, my dear Ritter, these are hardly normal circumstances.'

'I begin to grow tired with this!' snapped Chevalier. 'What are you talking about?'

'Well, for one thing,' Geis pointed out, 'you will notice that the machine guns in the hands of my men are pointing not, as you might expect, at the prisoners . . . but at you.'

An astonished glance confirmed that what Geis was saying was true, and Chevalier's mouth fell open. 'What in the name of the devil is this?'

'I don't know that there's a German word that quite covers it,' Geis told him, lazily. 'But the Americans have a good phrase: a set-up.'

'What?'

'What, indeed, *Herr Oberstgruppenführer?* You really were incredibly obvious, you know.'

'You . . . you're British?'

'Indeed I am,' Geis said.

'We all are. Allow me to introduce myself,' he smilingly parodied Chevalier's own words. 'My name is

David Smith. My rank and my precise occupation I think we'll skip. Suffice it to say that it involves watching the watchers – as we have been watching you, my dear Ritter, for some considerable time. Oh, forgive me, these gentlemen in the SS uniforms are, from left to right, Christian Zittwitz, Rolf Schmitz, Bodo Baumann and Franz Harenberg. Like Fräulein Renner, they work for Britain inside Germany.'

'I don't believe it!' Chevalier snapped.

'Understand me very clearly, my treacherous friend,' Smith said, an edge on his voice that chilled Chevalier to the marrow. 'You had better believe everything I tell you from this moment on, or you'll be dogmeat before you can heil Hitler!'

'Your threats are empty, Geis, or Smith, or whatever your name is. Don't you know I have already informed Gestapo headquarters that you are here to be taken? They will probably be here any moment!' Smith shook his head sadly.

'No chance, Ritter,' he said. 'Where do you think we got these uniforms? Where do you think I got *Hauptsturmführer* Geis's credentials?'

He let the message sink in, and then went on, 'Geis and his bully boys are tied up in the cellar. I've plans for them – and you.'

Chevalier shook his head, watching in stunned astonishment as Baumann proceeded to untie Jutta Renner, and the girl stood up, pushing the chair away, her eyes no longer soft and friendly but filled with contempt and hatred.

'How . . . ?' he managed.

'How?' Smith said. 'Well, I suppose you're entitled to know. Condemned man's breakfast, and all that. Ritter, you've been kidded, hoodwinked, bamboozled. We've been watching you for a year, waiting for you to make your move. At first, it was just a feeling we had, a malaise. Then suddenly, you "lost" three of your agents, and we sat up. It was when you put up the feasibility study for Operation Seelze that you showed your hand, requesting the kind of people you did, people you ought not to have known existed. So we decided to play you like a fish, Ritter. And you took the bait. Oh, how you swallowed it!'

'Damn you!' hissed Chevalier. 'Damn you!'

'I have only one regret, Ritter,' Smith continued, unperturbed by the outburst. 'There was no way I could prevent you from killing Sergeant Richardson. That was my miscalculation. I should have known you'd want the radio rendered useless right from the start. What happened, did Richardson put up a fight?'

'Not much of one,' sneered Chevalier.

'Well, you'll no doubt have that added to your bill at the end,' Smith said. 'We knew that it was your messages in advance which made it possible for the Manchester to fly in and out unmolested. They didn't need the plane, after all. They'd have you to tell them about it. But you must have been surprised when you got to the barn at Eilvese and found no welcoming committee.'

He turned to the others. 'The *Herr Oberst* didn't know, of course, that I was in the same plane, and had arranged a rendezvous with our four friends here. We had a little trouble with the squad that had been sent to capture you. But not much.' He allowed himself a faint smile.

'He nearly got away with something on the train to Seelze. He slipped a note to the Gestapo agent who was searching the train telling him to contact the authorities in Seelze and have you picked up at the station. He was probably bewildered when you arrived here, and again there was no reception committee.'

'How did you find out about the note?' Whitehead asked, speaking for the first time since Smith had revealed his identity.

'Perhaps Jutta would like to tell you that little story,' he said, softly.

'We in the Resistance had heard,' she began, faltering a little as Ritter glared at her use of the word 'resistance'; 'had heard,' she went on, more strongly now, defiance in her expression, 'that the Gestapo was deporting Jewish people. In Baden and Saarpfalz, 6,500. In Karlsruhe, Saarbrücken, many more. They were sent for internment in France, but we feared a more sinister motive. It has been the stated purpose of the Nazis to remove all Jews from German soil for some time. So our people have watched carefully for evidence that a round-up was planned, and informed Control. At the time when the people you saw on the station platform were being dragged from their homes, we were told. Fortunately for us – and for the people who had been arrested – we had expert help.'

She looked at Smith, who picked up the thread of her story. 'To cut a long story short,' he said, 'the *Schutzpolizei* and the Gestapo man in charge of them had a very nasty accident on the outskirts of Wunstorf. The Gestapo man and two policemen were killed, and I believe the others ran for their lives, abandoning their prisoners, who took advantage of their good fortune and promptly disappeared. I found the note in the dead Gestapo agent's coat. In fact, I'm wearing it.'

The smile that changed his craggy face so completely,

appeared for a moment, but then he grew serious again.

'Ritter was desperate, now. No one to take you at Seelze. He simply had to split you up, so he sent you on reconnaissances you really didn't need to make. His real job was to contact Fräulein Renner – and he knew how – and to get word into Gestapo headquarters. Both of which he did. With all of you captured or dead or both, of course, he would then have returned to London, reported that the mission had been a failure, and gone on with his spying for the *Abwehr*. Right, Ritter?'

'You're a fool, Smith,' Ritter rasped. 'There's no way you can get out of Seelze alive.'

'Wrong again,' Smith told him. 'My, my, you do make a habit of it, don't you? We have to do what we came to do first, of course. But we'll get clear.'

'I'd be interested to know how,' Ritter sneered.

'I'll bet you would,' Smith said. Then, without warning, he brought his hand over and down in a wicked chopping motion, the barrel of the Walther he had drawn while Ritter was speaking smacking with a sound like a butcher's axe hitting a side of beef at the point just above Ritter's right ear. The man went down with a crash that shook the building. Smith looked down at the fallen form dispassionately, then bent to check Ritter's pulse. It was slow, but regular. Apart from the slight trickle of blood sliding down behind his ear, Ritter was unmarked.

'All right,' Smith snapped. 'Tie him up, Bodo.' He turned to the others, who stood waiting expectantly, smiling.

'Well, David,' Whitehead said. 'It worked.'

'That it did,' Smith said. 'Let's hope everything else does!'

10

The truth of it was that every member of Chevalier's team was an imposter. George Davidson was no more connected with MO9's Commandos than Ken Whitehead was with Porton Down; the former no more a commissioned officer in His Majesty's armed forces than the latter was a physicist. And Miller: Smith smiled. If Dusty had really wanted to do anything with that transformer, he could probably have blown every fuse in Seelze. No, their skills, although specialist indeed, were not the ones which Chevalier had specified, their purpose not solely the one for which they had been so carefully briefed at Bovingdon. They were Smith's team, picked by him, and they had been given their real briefing several days before they had climbed into the Manchester to be flown out over Germany. In fact, the whole elaborate scheme had been born just before Christmas, shortly after Smith had submitted his report on Chevalier to the Chairman, the head of the National Security Executive.

The NSE was the most powerful and authoritative body in Britain. It had been set up to take control of, and already had complete central supervisory powers over, all British agencies specifically concerned with national security. It had been established shortly after the first intelligence reports received by the Government had indicated the likelihood of a German invasion in 1940.

The Chairman, and his two principal secretaries, were the real power behind the secret service. And the man they had selected to be their executive arm had been David Smith.

They had wanted a man who could, if necessary, put together an assault team of investigators who would not be troubled by the niceties of looking into the private life of an old school chum ; a man who knew, as much as any man could, the ramifications of international crime ; a man who would, when required, either lead an assassination team or himself execute an enemy of the state; a man who was able, constantly, to watch the watchers themselves. The Chairman was aware – only too aware, since they had nicknamed him 'the Butcher of MI5' – of the distrust and rivalry which existed between MI5, which was responsible for counter-espionage on British soil, and MI6 (or SIS) which was mainly concerned with foreign subversion. MI5 were openly contemptuous (often with very good reason) of the security in SIS, while SIS advocated – with equally good reason – that MI5 hadn't the remotest idea what espionage was all about. With the possibility of invasion imminent and the risk of internal subversion as high as it was in the first year of the war, the Chairman had taken no chances. Smith had been established in a small office at 8 Bow Churchyard, just off Cheapside, with a forbidding secretary named Mrs Phillips, who had been supplied by the Foreign Office. She was a large, grey-haired, middle-aged lady of such formidable mien that he had never yet dared to ask her Christian name. She looked with a disdain bordering upon contempt on all of Smith's visitors, whether they were British or 'shifty foreigners' – her epithet for some of the seedier characters who crossed his threshold.

The Chairman had chosen well, and he fought for Smith, although his advisers had reservations from the start. To begin with, although Smith had been born, raised and educated in England, the fellow was half-Italian. Yes, they admitted that Eton and Winchester were impeccable background references, and yes, they agreed that Sir Anthony Smith had been a respected and much-admired member of the landed gentry in leafy Bucks, and also a gallant soldier who had certainly earned the DSO he won at Vimy Ridge. But Sir Anthony was dead and the widow Smith had returned to her native Sicily where, it was understood, she had married some local Don. There were hints – no more – that he was connected with the *mafia* but, as the Chairman pointed out, not an atom of proof. Besides, he added, Smith's mother's marital arrangements had no relevance to his fitness for the job or otherwise. His advisers had persisted, however. Did he know, for instance, that Smith was reputed to be a mercenary? That there were grounds for suspecting he had been responsible for penetrating the plot to assassinate General Metaxas, the dictator of Greece, in January 1938? No proof, the Chairman gently pointed out. Then how about the part he was said to have played in the flight to Greece of King Zog of Albania in April, 1939? To his credit if true, the Chairman had adjudged; but again, not a jot, not a tittle of proof. What about the rumours that Smith had lived off the proceeds of gun-running into Abyssinia during the Italian invasion three years ago? The Chairman stopped them, brushing aside their objections. Rumour, guesswork, hearsay all of it. If what they said was true, then Smith was extraordinarily adept at concealing his tracks and would, by definition, be able to spot anyone else doing the same thing. If – and the *if* stressed – he had connexions with the underworld, they would be valuable, since it was well known that in most of the criminal cases cracked by the police they were acting on information received from that very source. If, as they claimed, Smith knew the dark and slimy regions of espionage and spying, who better to watch the men whom Britain charged with those tasks ?

In the end, the Chairman had his way, and the 'consultancy' was established. Nominally, Smith was available to any Ministry as an expert in propaganda methods, and one of his first commissions had been to come up with a slogan for a poster to be circulated by the Ministry of Information at all military bases, airfields and army camps, as well as other places of general assembly like pubs, cinemas, railway stations and bus termini. Since Smith's *forte,* whatever it was, certainly wasn't advertising slogans, he called in a friend in the publicity business who came up with the slogan 'Careless Talk Costs Lives' and *David Smith, (Consultant) Ltd* was on its way with a credit it had hardly earned. His real work, however, was tougher ; and his credits, when they came, were earned the hard way.

The first job was to vet the dossiers of the original staff of a new branch of MI6 called Special Operations Executive, formed by Cabinet order in July, 1940. Using contacts—and methods—which would have appalled the NSE, they looked in dark corners NSE would have shuddered to know existed for venery they could not conceive. Smith was responsible for making sure that at least three potential traitors never got anywhere near Norgeby House.

The second assignment, a much more unpleasant one, was to investigate the overall running of MI5, whose systems and methods he found in such appalling disarray — outside MI5's headquarters, the bus conductors were shouting to the leggy debs alighting to go to work inside 'All chinge for the secret service!'—that NSE made the very strongest representations to the Cabinet and, in short order, there was drastic change at the very top. The inevitable chain-reaction had earned the Chairman his nickname, but he knew it really belonged to Smith.

The third 'consultation' began in much the same way as all the others. The telephone rang, and Mrs Phillips snatched it away before he could touch it. When the caller announced himself, she looked at Smith the way secretaries sometimes look at bosses who are taking calls from their mistresses while the work is piling up.

'It's him,' she said.

'Smith.'

'David ? Philip. Call the Annexe at 10.30. Sharp.'

Before Smith had even time to acknowledge the phone went dead and he was left staring at it. He looked at his watch. Nine forty-five.

'I have to go out, Mrs Phillips,' he said. 'I'll be back about eleven.'

'Yes, sir,' she said, disbelief in every syllable. He tried for a smile, and failed miserably. Shrugging into his overcoat, he went down the narrow stairs, hearing the busy chatter of typewriters in Beeton's, the shipping agents, and out into the street. It was like some weird, unearthly ruined land. In the blitz which had begun the preceding autumn, much of the area around St Paul's had been razed by German bombs, the ruins gutted by the biggest fire since the one which had destroyed the

City in 1666. On some of the older bombed-sites, weeds were already running rank and wild. Somewhere far away he could hear the steady clanging of a fire-engine bell. But the City was living as normal a life as was possible. It might take a week to get a letter delivered half a mile away. It might be necessary to queue for anything up to two hours behind seventy people to get on a sixty-seater trolleybus that might anyway have been diverted to a totally different route. It might not be possible to cook your food, because the gas or electricity was cut off. You might not be able to get in to see *Gone with the Wind* at the Empire. You might have to spend most nights of the week in the damp, muggy confinement of your air raid shelter or under the stairs or down the Underground. You might have sent your kids 'on evacuation'. You might get yelled at by an ARP warden for lighting a cigarette in the street at night : 'Put that bloody light out!' But you kept smiling. The most popular saying of the day was 'Britain can take it!' And taking it Britain most certainly was, Smith reflected as he hurried around St Paul's Churchyard and down Ludgate Hill. By 10.15, he was comfortably ensconced in his usual chair, by the serving hatch to the rear room of El Vino's, a bottle of Sancerre in front of him. Wine was one of Smith's weaknesses and they were saving these last few bottles for him. When they ran out, he'd have to do the best he could, he supposed. Like everyone else. At ten-thirty, he went to the telephone in the corner. Although it was often the case that you couldn't even get through to the Exchange these days, El Vino's — patron pub of newspapermen — was a sacrosanct number, and any breaks in the line were hastily repaired, it being considered in the national interest to ensure that newspapermen could be sure of one watering-hole from which to phone in their front-line stories.

He dialled WHI 5422 at 10.29 precisely.

The burr of the ringing tone sounded only once and then a brisk, clipped voice said, 'Duty Officer.'

'Smith,' he said. 'For the Chairman.'

'Oh, yes, sir,' said the disembodied voice. 'I have a message for you. You are to be here at eleven, sir.'

'At the Annexe?'

'That is correct, sir.'

He hung up, a faint frown of surprise on his battered face. Still, there was no time to worry about the unusual command. He told the girl at the bar to put the rest of the Sancerre on ice for Eric, his contact on the *Standard,* who kept him informed on developments in the newspaper and publishing business. Eric was an El Vino regular, and Smith knew he would be in at eleven. He went out, saying goodbye to the girls who were just getting ready to open up. His arrangement to use the place for the half hour prior to opening on any day was one of long standing, and had been arranged by someone who didn't need to worry if one or two licensing laws were bent in the process. He was lucky this morning. A taxi was unloading a fare at the foot of Chancery Lane, and he ran for it, telling the driver to take him to Storey's Gate.

The blue-uniformed lift attendant, his MoD lapel badges brightly shined, took him down the thirty-five feet to the Annexe. Here, deep beneath the Ministry of Defence building, worked a staff of almost three hundred people – people who seldom saw daylight but worked, ate, slept and, for all Smith knew, married and had babies in the foetid, pumped-air atmosphere which the languid fans lazily rearranged. Here was the nerve centre of War Command – the huge Map Room with its forest of red and green scrambler phones, its huge wall maps speckled and spattered with pins and flags of every conceivable size, the desk of the Duty Officer who made daily reports, the clocks showing the different times around the world: Washington, Tokyo, Berlin, Sydney, Rome. Off on the opposite side of the corridor was Churchill's cell-like office-cum-bedroom, and further along the *sanctum sanctorum* – Room 63 with its legend *Keep Locked,* and the sign above the door which said, that there was a key with the Map Room Duty Officer. Only Churchill himself was allowed inside this room, but it never occurred to anyone to question why; for on the door was a 'Vacant-Engaged' lock such as is found on any public lavatory. Smith, however, knew that inside the 'Engaged' sign was showing, Churchill was on the Washington time, and a telephone with a direct line to the White House there. Its code name was 'X-ray' and the scrambler it required was so big that it was stored in the cellar of an Oxford Street department store. When the 'Engaged' sign was showing, Churchil was on the phone to President Roosevelt, with whom he regularly discussed Britain's progress, or lack of it, in the war.

Now, however, Smith was taken directly to the Cabinet room and shown in. There were only two men there: the Chairman and the Prime Minister. Both looked grave. The Chairman motioned Smith to take a seat and went on with his low-pitched conversation with the Prime Minister. It wasn't a pretty room. Utilitarian, Smith thought, from the trestle tables covered with black-out blanketing to the tubular steel chairs and the

Geographia maps on the wall. Churchill had the only wooden chair, and it was decidedly far from new. Behind it stood two fire buckets full of sand, which the old man used for ashtrays. Both were plugged full of cigar butts.

'All right,' Churchill said. His familiar, gruff voice carried the ring of someone who has been convinced against his will. He pressed a button on the table in front of him and a bell rang outside. Smith heard the sound of the double doors being locked and the stamp of the Marine sentries' feet in the corridor outside.

'This is David Smith, Prime Minister,' The Chairman said. 'I told you about him.'

Smith came to attention in front of the table, and Churchill frowned at him, lips clamped on his cigar, not an ounce of friendliness in his eyes or his face.

'Hmph,' he said.

'I think the Prime Minister is convinced of the necessity of acting on our plan, David,' the Chairman said, the faintest hint of a frosty smile touching his mouth. 'Now I want you to explain it to him fully.'

'And briefly,' Churchill scowled, using a Swan Vesta to relight his cigar. He puffed huge clouds of smoke, never taking his red-rimmed eyes off Smith as he listened to the plan which Smith had put together during the long, sleepless nights after he had discovered Chevalier was a traitor. It involved deception on a fairly large scale, but a necessary deception for all that. It involved dispensations only the Prime Minister – or his Cabinet – could give. And it involved a high factor of risk; although Smith was ready and willing to accept it, he could not commit all those whom he would need to co-operate with him without Churchill's assent.

'Dirty business,' Churchill growled, shaking his great head. 'Never liked it.'

'What we have in mind, Winston,' the Chairman said gently. 'Is making it a shade cleaner.' He let the frosty smile appear like a ghost for a moment. 'If only a shade,' he added.

'Hmph,' Churchill said. He glowered at Smith as though daring him to say anything. Smith said nothing.

'All right,' Churchill said. 'Let me have it in writing.'

He jabbed the wet butt of the cigar towards Smith, pointing with it. 'As for you,' he added. 'Good luck.'

All of it came back to him now as they sat in a tight circle in the cellar of the *Bäckerei* Renner – his team, Whitehead, on detachment from the Explosives Research and Development Establishment at the Royal Ordnance Factory, Davidson, on detachment from the Royal Military Police, and Miller, on detachment from H.M. Prison, Parkhurst, Isle of Wight. Smith had known Whitehead long before the war, in the days when he had had an international reputation as the most reliable, most inventive, explosives expert in Europe. There was nothing about them, or about firearms, that Whitehead did not know, and he was an astonishing innovator. It had been said of him that, given a packet of sulphur tablets and a box of toy caps, Whitehead could have blown open the vault of the Bank of England ; and he was a 'natural' with any kind of gun – from a beaten-up Frontier Colt to a howitzer. George Davidson had been brought to Smith's attention shortly after Dunkirk, and he had read the astonishing report of how the dour-faced Scot, cut off from his retreating regiment, had attacked a German forward command post single-handed, killing everyone in it, appropriating their entire supply of hand-grenades, two machine-pistols and a pair of Lugers, and shot his way through an area in which it was later estimated that there had been upwards of 6,000 crack Waffen SS. Fitness reports and other accounts which Smith had had sent him, showed that Davidson was as 'natural' in his own field as was Whitehead in his. The difference was that Davidson had not made a profession out of the fact that he was a born fighter and a ruthlessly efficient killing machine. Miller — well, Miller was what he acted like. The little Cockney was in Parkhurst because it was the only prison that was certainly proof against his dexterous, supple fingers and his unsurpassed skill at picking locks, by passing alarm systems, and — perhaps most important of all, where this mission was concerned — given suitable tools and preparation, possessed of an uncanny ability to make anything electrical sit up and beg. There had been a round-the-clock guard on his cell in Parkhurst when Smith had gone to see Miller. The little man had jumped at the chance he was offered: freedom, on condition. Anything was better than sitting staring at the greasy walls of the maximum security block. Besides, as Miller had aggrievedly pointed out to Smith, the cells were full of bloody foreigners.

There was no German Resistance, of course. The four 'Germans' were in fact Poles who had volunteered to work behind the lines in Germany. They had their own special reasons for wanting revenge on the Gestapo. They were the names of cities like Stettin, Teschen, Cracow, and many others on the roll of infamy that was beginning in the Third Reich, the first awful stirring of what history would remember as 'the final solution' of Germany's Jewish 'problem'.

He shook off his wool-gathering mood. There was much to be done, and very little time to do it.

'Gentlemen – and lady,' he said, with a smile at Jutta Renner. 'Let's get down to business.'

I I

The raid on Seelze was launched at precisely 3.15.

Every man in it had gone over and over his role until he was letter-and-time-perfect. He knew when to run, when to walk, and where there was a little fat on his timetable so he could stop and think. Smith gravely shook hands with every one of them, and at 2.15 he slapped Zittwitz and Baumann on the shoulder.

They left quickly, their destination the left-luggage office at the station where they would pick up the haversacks and small suitcases which had been left there earlier that day. It took them less than ten minutes more to clip unobtrusively through the lock-chains on two bicycles standing in the metal rack on the forecourt, and another two to reach the Wunstorferstrasse, where they turned west, heading along towards the point where the road swung to the right prior to crossing the bridge across the canal.

Harenberg and Schmitz were next. They swung the heavy packs Smith had provided on to their backs, Harenberg also carrying a draw-stringed sack in his hand. They had forty-five minutes to find, steal, and drive away any armed heavy vehicle they could lay their hands on. It took them only fourteen of those forty minutes to discover a 3-ton pursuit vehicle parked in the space between two shops on the Schulstrasse. There was no sign of its crew, and it took Schmitz about thirty seconds to wire the ignition and get the engine turning. He jumped up into the steel-sided well at the rear, taking his seat behind the 7.92 mm Spandau mounted on a swivel there, as Harenberg eased the vehicle out into the street, turning left up the Kirchstrasse to their first destination.

Whitehead and Davidson left at 2.45.

'You know what to do?' Smith asked again.

'We know,' Davidson replied.

'Good luck,' Smith repeated.

'Same to you,' was the terse reply. They eased out of the doorway as Jutta Renner opened it and, with a tight smile, both men were gone. The girl looked at Smith expectedly.

'And now?' she whispered.

'And now – we wait,' he said, knowing that it was the hardest thing of all to do. Even Miller, squatting in the corner, muffled in the Waffen SS uniform, didn't have any funny stories to tell today.

'Won't someone come looking for Geis?' he asked, after a while.

'No reason they should,' Smith said. 'The man's a Staff Officer, and had plenty of assistance. Probably didn't even let anyone know he was coming to take us – wanted the glory all to himself.'

'Let's hope you're right,' Miller said fervently. 'We'd be in trouble if they sent another squad over here to look for him.'

Smith smiled, his battered face almost handsome.

'You think we're not in trouble now, Dusty?' he asked, mischievously.

There was no answer to that one.

At 3.05, Harenberg and Schmitz clambered back into the driving seat and gunner's seat respectively of the pursuit vehicle, their work at the Leinebrucke, the bridge across the river at the northern edge of the town, done. They rolled the car without haste into the Wiesenweg, and down the Goethestrasse to the corner of the Schulstrasse. At 3.09, Zittwitz and Baumann trundled up from the Wunstorferstrasse on their bicycles, leaning them against the blank wall of a garage on the corner and ambling unobtrusively across to the PV. Clambering aboard, they swung their haversacks to the bed of the gun box at the back, loosening the fastenings on the top.

At 3.12 precisely, a camouflaged staff car with an open top slid to a silent halt behind the parked PV. Davidson got out of the Mercedes and walked to where he could see Harenberg in the driver's cab.

'All set?' he asked.

Harenberg nodded. The muscles of his thick neck were corded with tension, and his knuckles were white where his hands clenched the wheel.

'All right, switch over,' Davidson said. Harenberg gave the word to Baumann, who swung out of the rear of the truck and took Davidson's place at the wheel beside Whitehead.

'Okay!' Davidson yelled, and Harenberg let in the clutch, the big three-tonner lurching forward, picking up speed fast as he jammed the accelerator to the floorboards and went barrelling across the Goethestrasse towards the drop-pole gate in front of the main admin. building of the factory complex.

He was hitting around fifty when he smashed through the pole, the sentry jumping for his life as the Mercedes behind the truck swerved, smashing down the sentry-box with its telephone link to the command post. The truck heeled over sharp right, roaring past the admin. building at almost sixty, skidding furiously to the left as Schmitz raked the ground floor windows of the admin. building with the heavy Spandau, the chattering stutter of the big machine-gun shockingly loud in the quiet afternoon. Something exploded inside the building with a flat hard crack, and a tongue of flame leaped from one of the windows, as Baumann jammed on the anchors of the Mercedes in the alleyway between the command post and the admin. building. Whitehead was already out and running, arm lobbing over in a smooth, sweet movement that sent the heavy, yellow-painted phosphorus grenade soaring up to smash through the window and explode inside with a searing blast of white flame. Without even breaking his stride, Whitehead was turning right and repeating his action, the grenade this time going through the doorway of the admin. building, its explosion shaking the place, glass and masonry bursting outwards, as he ran to catch the car and Baumann slammed it into movement around the front of the larger, general admin. building. Whitehead, kneeling on the seat of the moving car, raked the windows of the building with his Schmeisser and then turned quickly as the guards from the sentry boxes at the front, facing the Wunstorferstrasse, ran shouting towards the Mercedes, unslinging their rifles as they came. Whitehead cut them down mercilessly as they roared along the gravelled path, Baumann wheeling the car right and coming to a rocking halt. Whitehead was already out of the car, with Baumann right on his heels, as guards began to spill out of the big guardroom building directly in front of them. Their two machine-pistols chattered, and the shouting, running men in front of them melted to the ground, torn apart by the scything hail of bullets. Now they were level with the south wall of the guardroom building, and Whitehead smacked in the window with the butt of his Schmeisser as Baumann jammed his own machine-pistol through the hole and pulled the trigger for a long searching burst. Then he jumped quickly back as Whitehead tossed one, two, three of the yellow grenades through the shattered glass. They both ran flat out for the car, diving behind it for shelter as the grenades exploded in the crowded building. There was an enormous tongue of flame, and then the whole place went up. The explosion was deafening, the pulsing roar of the bursting grenades pressing like strong fingers on their eardrums, as they lay flat on the ground with their heads beneath their arms.

'One up for Wigan,' Whitehead said. Then he scrambled to his feet and ran towards the general admin. building.

Harenberg was doing forty by the time the pursuit vehicle was level with the south-western corner of the hulking effluent plant, and the Spandau kept up its incessant, bludgeoning chatter as Schmitz raked the windows and walls of the buildings on both sides. Half-way along the alley, Davidson steadied himself with one hand on the roof of the rocking vehicle, his arm moving as he tossed grenade after bursting grenade through the gaping, shattered windows on both sides.

'*Achtung!*' screamed Schmitz, as Harenberg wheeled the big three-tonner into a swerve, smacking into the rear of a small car parked at the rear of the admin. building. The pursuit vehicle shuddered at the smashing impact, and the buckled bonnet sprang half-open, but the impetus of the collision nearly flattened the smaller car, whacking it around, ripping off the tyres with a screech and a stink of burning rubber, and rolling the car over against another, which stopped the movement dead. The collision split open the petrol tank of the first car, and as Schmitz raked the shattered vehicles with the Spandau, the splattering petrol ignited with a dull whoompf, and in a moment the flames were spreading across the entire parking area, a huge cloud of black smoke spiralling skywards to join the flickering flames from the effluent plant and the general admin. building into which Davidson had lobbed his grenades.

At the corner of the admin. building Harenberg jammed on the brakes, spilling them all forward. To their left, the guardroom building was burning furiously, and there were men running everywhere. Sirens were adding their whooping alarum to the confusion as Schmitz swung his Spandau around in a tight half circle, raking the three alleyways that the pursuit vehicle was spraddling. Davidson and Zittwitz were already out of the vehicle, running north up the alley between the laboratory and the big stock warehouse. Every ten yards, Davidson stopped and lobbed one of the yellow grenades in through the shattered window where, moments before, Zittwitz had poked the barrel of his machine-pistol and raked the interior. Behind them, Schmitz was handling the Spandau with a feral grin of vengeful hate on his face, screaming curses as he poured a lashing hail of lead into the roiling smoke, cutting down running men the moment they appeared. The dull, repetitive boom of explosions and chain-explosions all around sent huge chunks of masonry, timber, smoke, flame, dust, and tattered things that might have been men skywards as Davidson veered left towards the railway lines which ended at the loading and unloading bays ahead. Zittwitz shouted a hoarse warning and went down on one knee, his burst of fire whacking three German soldiers off their feet as they came running around the corner of the building.

'Dogs!' Zittwitz yelled, and Davidson reacted blindly, jerking the trigger of his snatched-out Walther, laying down a panicked hail of fire at the animals that were blurring at him across the empty concrete. There was an agonised yelp from one of them, and another went up into the air in a contorted arc, coming down flat dead on the ground. The wounded one swerved away, body low as it ran terrified from the unseen thing that had hurt it.

Now Davidson went into the open on the far side of the entrance to the loading bay, his heart jumping when he saw the locomotive standing there, hissing gently, unattended beneath the overhanging roof of the building. He waved an arm to Zittwitz to tell him to come on, then ran flat and hard across the space between himself and the engine, sliding to a panting halt beside it, and edging along towards the footplate. There was no one there, so he vaulted up on to the footplate, checking over the controls in the cab. The huge control lever was set at neutral, and the heavy brake was on. He jerked off the brake and, with a huge surge of power, lifted the control lever into the reverse position. The loco shuddered, all its power concentrated on the drive shafts simultaneously, wheels chattering and grinding on the rails as it shivered into motion, moving slowly backwards, colliding with the wagons behind it and making a long, jangling chain of noise that could be heard above the smashing thuds of the explosions in the complex. Stripping off four fuses, Davidson jammed grenades up against the foot of the control box and skipped off on the side, using his impetus to take him running towards the generator room at the rear of the laboratory, waving to Zittwtz to cover him as he ran.

Zittwitz was just two seconds too late to kill the soldier who ran out from the far side of the laboratory. The man knelt quickly and shot Davidson through the body, and the big Scot fell, his body tensed with agony, rolling instinctively for cover as Zittwitz shot down the German and another who had run out to join him.

Now Zittwitz stood in an agony of momentary indecision. The orders were strict, capable of no interpretation. You were not to stop for anyone who fell. If you didn't make the rendezvous, the others assumed you dead and left without you. There were no second chances.

All this went through his mind in the half second he stood there, and then, with a sort of shrug, he ran flat out across the open space to where the fallen man lay. He dragged Davidson back behind the transformer hut, turning fast to rake the area he had just crossed with the machine pistol.

'Jes–*us*.' Davidson managed. '*Down!*'

Almost as if his word had been a trigger, there was a massive explosion on the far side of the complex. The trundling locomotive was almost level with the middle of the huge warehouse facing the tracks, when the four grenades went off simultaneously. They tore the belly out of the huge locomotive, and great tearing, whistling hunks of boiling hot steel whistled upwards and outwards. They smashed into the walls and windows of the warehouse just a fraction of a second ahead of the great ball of fire from the grenades, which licked across the devastated fifty-square yard area on which the train had been standing, setting fire to boxes inside the building, and driving men who had been hiding inside fleeing in panic. They knew what was stored in the warehouse. They knew what would happen if any of the canisters in there exploded. Almost two hundred tons of tear gas being exploded simultaneously was not something any sane man wanted to witness. They ran like rabbits, leaving perhaps a dozen guards furiously battling the reaching flames.

'Get,' Davidson said to the smaller man crouching alongside him. 'Out.'

Zittwitz looked at the tall Scot. The front of his body was covered in a heaving mass of black blood and torn flesh ; the bullet had gone through from back to front and there was no way he was going to be able to get Davidson out.

'Go,' Davidson hissed, and then, when Zittwitz hesitated, he found the strength to heave himself up, back against the wall of the hut.

'Give me that damned gun !' Davidson gritted. 'Then get going ! That's an order !'

He snatched the Schmeisser out of Zittwitz' hands, gave him a faltering push. 'And . . . luck,' he managed. He even tried for a grin, but a surge of pain turned his face white and empty.

'Luck,' Zittwitz said. Then he eased out into the alley between the lab. and the warehouse, and ran as hard and as fast as he could to where the pursuit vehicle still stood at the crossroads, waiting for them.

From the moment they had burst through the drop-poles, the entire raid had so far consumed exactly nine minutes.

When the research laboratory complex had been established at Seelze, late in 1940, *Sturmbannführer* Klaus Flugge had taken his job of making it secure against sabotage or bombing very seriously. He had set up an elaborate and comprehensive set of security measures designed to cover most eventualities that might occur, measures designed to do two things: one, to protect the valuable person of the leading member of the research team, Dr Karl Heineman; and two, to ensure that the valuable research documents upon which Heineman was working were never likely to fall into the wrong hands. If, third, he also planned to ensure the continued survival of *Sturmbannführer* Klaus Flugge, he did not think that remiss of him. The Reich had no need of a dead hero.

To be sure, even *Sturmbannführer* Flugge had not anticipated the suicidal ferocity of the raid which had finally happened, but he had covered every other eventuality. Every week, for instance, he had held drills at the main administration building, drills which involved the people it would be necessary to safeguard in the event of any attempt to penetrate the complex.

They consisted of himself, Dr Karl Heineman, Dr Hans Gessler (Heineman's assistant), and the two picked SS troopers who were always on guard outside Heineman's and his own office doors. When the sirens sounded their shrieking alarm, they fell into the routine as though they had been doing it every day for weeks, and he smiled thinly as he watched the hasty preparations. The two SS guards stood by the doors, cocked machine-pistols ready to shoot anything or anyone moving in the corridor. As the building rocked with the explosions of Whitehead's grenades below, Gessler swung the heavy metal box from beneath the desk, snapping it open as, with precise movements, Heineman and he stacked their research papers into it. Even with hands trembling with haste and fear, the two men had the job done in three minutes, and Flugge now waved his men forward. They ran ahead of the two scientists, with Flugge bringing up the rear, Luger cocked in his hand. Downstairs in the hall, a man lay dead, his body compressed and twisted in a strangely distorted way, killed by the blast of the grenades which had torn half of the southern wall of the building away. Beyond the shattered partitions they could see a huge roaring wall of white flame that already gave off an enormous, skin-cracking heat.

The two guards ran out into the open, checking to right and to left, machine-pistols cocked for action, but there were only a few men in sight, and those were running towards the sound of firing and explosions they could hear behind them, deep inside the complex.

'The car! Quick, quick, damn you!' shouted Flugge, as he herded the two scientists across the open ground to where his own Mercedes was parked on the verge in front of the building. Above the noise of the sirens and the unceasing rumble of explosions, he could hear another sound, the dull par-pee-par-pee of klaxons and smiled. Another of his systems had been to arrange an underground cable alarm system between the factory complex and the *Hauptamt*. In the event of any alarm, troops could be at the factories within ten minutes of the alarm's sounding.

'Get out of here, man!' he shouted, banging the SS guard who had slid into the driving seat on the shoulder. Heineman and Gessler were huddled in the back, the former's thin arms wrapped around the heavy steel box as though protecting it. The second SS guard knelt between them, his Schmeisser covering their rear across the folded hood of the open car. They skidded into the Schulstrasse as the first armoured car, the heavy lorries in line behind it packed with troops, roared across the Goethestrasse towards the plant.

Whitehead had finished placing his explosives, and was coming out of the admin. building at a flat run, when Baumann let out a hoarse yell. He had already backed and turned the car, and was waiting now with the engine roaring, counting down in his mind to the moment when the pursuit vehicle would come roaring down the alleyway between the devastated guardroom building and the soon-to-go – if Whitehead was as good as they said – general admin. building. What he hadn't reckoned on was seeing half of the German army come slewing around the far end of the general administration building. The leading vehicle was a pursuit car, whose driver skidded it into a beautiful raking curve that brought him sideways-on to the Mercedes, and in the best of all positions for the machine-gunner on the rear to rake the unprotected vehicle with the Spandau. Behind him lorries full of soldiers spread outwards and the grey coated figures came off the tail-boards like ants.

Baumann turned loose with the Schmeisser, feeling like a kid taking on an elephant with a pea shooter, then vaulted over the rear of the car and ran in a long arc towards the fence fronting the complex, desperately drawing the Spandau gunner's attention away from the Mercedes. He hit the ground in a diving roll as the Germans cut loose at his dodging waving figure, almost crying out with relief as he saw, in a blur of movement, that the pursuit vehicle driven by Harenberg had just skidded around the corner. From the rear gun position, Schmitz had a beautiful profile shot at the German who was just depressing his own machine-gun to pick off Baumann. Schmitz jerked the trigger with a yell of triumph and his blast of fire tore the German gunner out of his seat and into a tattered heap on the far side of the vehicle. The driver slammed to one side as the bullets shattered the windows of the cab, and Schmitz kept swinging the gun in a tight arc, right and left, that kept the entire German force with their heads down. Baumann now made a desperate run back towards the Mercedes in this moment of grace, but he hadn't covered half of the distance when a volley of shots spun him off his feet in a welter of arms and legs. He ploughed into the gravel, face down, and lay unmoving.

The flames roaring inside the general administration building suddenly belched with renewed vigour, and a great black cloud of oily smoke momentarily obscured the massed Germans at the far end.

'Let's get the hell out of here!' shouted Whitehead. He leaped on board the pursuit car and banged on the roof, snatching up a machine-gun, and adding his fire-power to the hail that Zittwitz and Schmitz were already pouring into the smoke. Harenberg slammed the car into gear and wheeled her over, heading like a bat out of hell for the drop-pole gate into the Wunstorferstrasse.

'God in Heaven!' shouted Zittwitz. 'Look at that!'

That was a three-ton armoured car, sitting squatly, like some prehistoric monster, across the feeder road leading into the Industriestrasse, and directly in their path. Harenberg slammed on the brakes, while Schmitz whirled the Spandau around towards this new source of peril. He did not pull the trigger : as well throw stones as try to dent a vehicle plated with steel like this, with even the heavy bullets of the Spandau.

Whitehead watched in frozen disbelief as the turret started to move. He could distinctly hear the gears inside the car as the gunner moved the long snout of the 75 mm cannon around to line up on them. They could almost see him squinting down the aiming sight, hand on the firing button. There wasn't a damned thing they could do but wait until he pressed it and blew them to Kingdom Come.

'All right,' Davidson said. 'All right.'

Everything felt light inside him now, his body all relaxed, loose, as if he could run a thousand miles without getting out of breath. If he also knew that, soon, the numbness below his breastbone would turn to searing agony, he was grateful to Death for at least giving him a breathing space to do what he wanted to do. His hands were slippery with the blood which had smeared on to them off his body, but he held tight on to the haversack lying across his legs.

'All right,' he panted again. He was having some trouble focussing his eyesight, and there was a high, keening buzz far away in the back of his head, but he knew that he had to get up and get going. He looked up. Directly opposite him stood the loading bay where he had started up the locomotive. It looked about a thousand miles away.

With an effort that took nearly all of his remaining strength, Davidson stood up, crouching so that his head did not project around the edge of the transformer hut, the inbuilt caution of many years protecting him from instinct rather than conscious thought.

'One,' he muttered, listening to the dull, crackling chatter of rifle or machine-gun fire somewhere, a long way away.

'Two,' he added, drawing in his breath and tensing his shuddering leg muscles. Then he nodded and, without saying the third number, ran weaving out into the open, across the naked concrete towards the towering hulk of the loading bay.

Immediately he was out in the open, the soldiers hidden behind the corner of the laboratories opened fire, and he felt as if someone had punched him hard in the back.

'Can't kill me,' he thought, eyes fixed on the corner of the wall ahead, nothing keeping him going but his own indomitable will. 'Dead already,' he added, making it to the shelter of the angle, sinking to his knees with the haversack a pillow for his drooping head. There was blood in his mouth, and he realized that he had run into the rough brick wall.

'Hell,' he managed.

It took the very last of his strength to make his legs carry him up the two stone steps and on to the loading platform. It was a wide, smooth, concrete area, with rolling shutter doors on the far side leading into the high-ceilinged receiving warehouse, stacked with huge crates of chemicals, equipment, oxygen and hydrogen cylinders. He staggered across the bay and into the warehouse, shaking his head to clear away the roaring red mists of pain. His hands slithered as he fumbled for the tapes on the grenades, coating them with blood, but he managed to rip them off and then stagger into the centre of the warehouse, where he sat down like some lolling marionette, swaying on the edge of a box with the word *Sprengstoff* stencilled on it. He held the haversack close to him, like a child clutching its favourite teddy bear, and he was smiling when the two German guards came running and stood in front of him, their machine-pistols trained on him.

'*Grüss Gott,*' he said, cheerfully, and then the bombs went off, making a blinding, searing, irresistible ball of fire which consumed everything within fifty feet and set off the most astonishing detonation of them all.

12

There was only one thing they could do, and Zittwitz did it. Even as the menacing snout of the armoured car began to swing around, he was moving at a tangent in a running crouch, covered from the machine-gunner in the car by the diagonally striped sentry-box, until he could make a quartering run at the side of the vehicle. The muzzle of the cannon was settled now, and Whitehead swore he heard the rattle of the breech in the same moment that Zittwitz lifted the hatch cover and slammed it down, leaping away frenziedly for safety, scrabbling for cover in the count of three.

Then the grenade went off inside the vehicle. There were slots in the front and at the sides, and they could see them lit as if by magnesium, an intense, almost blinding light. The top of the armoured car sprang open like a ruptured can and the vehicle tilted to one side, suddenly enveloped in a mass of flames, every man in it killed instantly.

'Go, go, go, go!' screamed Whitehead, slamming the flat of his hand on the top of the driver's cab, as Harenberg jammed the gears in and banged down the accelerator. The pursuit car leaped forward, the soldiers on the far side of the burning admin. building rushing out with a hoarse yell of rage, firing haphazardly at the moving vehicle, which lurched around the blazing armoured car. Zittwitz came running alongside and was hoisted aboard by main force as Harenberg tooled the car out on to the Wunstorferstrasse, turning right and pushing the vehicle as hard as it would go.

It was then, finally, that the charges Whitehead had laid around the general administration building exploded simultaneously, destroying the entire west wing and burying the vehicles roaring into pursuit in a huge avalanche of falling masonry, burning wood, and roaring yellow flame.

'Go, go!' Whitehead shouted against the wind, his face a grinning, sooty mask of devilish delight. Way behind them, he could see more cars coming along the straight road running alongside the canal, but they were about a half mile back. With luck – and so far they'd had all the luck – they'd make it to the bridge with time to spare. He crouched down, and looked at Zittwitz, who was slumped on the bed of the pursuit vehicle, his face drained and empty.

Whitehead clapped him on the shoulder, and shook him gently, a way of saying 'well done'. But Zittwitz shook his head and turned away still seeing George Davidson's pain-wracked face, trying for a grin as he'd wished him luck for the last time.

The big Mercedes squealed to a halt in the deserted street outside the Gestapo *Hauptamt,* and *Sturmbann-führer* Flugge checked his watch with a satisfied nod. Eight minutes. Two more, and Heineman and his precious papers would be in the concrete bunker beneath the Gestapo building, safe from anything, even a direct hit from the biggest bomb the British had. The SS guard on the passenger side jumped out, his boot heels echoing on the empty pavement, Schmeisser at the port as he wheeled to open the rear door. Flugge was leaning forward when he heard a sound, for all the world like a polite cough, that was so familiar he did not recognize it until he saw the big guard torn off his feet by the bullet from the silenced gun, his head hitting the pavement with an awful, final sound.

Whirling to see the big, ugly man with the pistol in his hand moving fast across the rear of the car, Flugge wrenched at the flap of his holstered pistol, but in that moment the grenade which the big man had tossed into the doorway of the Gestapo *Hauptamt* exploded with a booming, cracking roar. The sentry, who had been starting forward to the car, was blasted flat, unconscious on his face, and Flugge was blown back into the car, sprawling heavily across the bodies of the astonished Heineman and Gessler.

The driver had been trying for the pistol at his side when the grenade went off, but the blast drove him off his seat and out into the road, sprawling there helplessly as Smith shot him dead without compunction. Smith leaped into the driving seat as Jutta Renner ran out across the street and got into the passenger side, the Walther pistol in her hand laid across the back of the seat and pointed directly at Flugge's forehead.

'You!' he cursed, struggling upright.

'Me!' she acknowledged.

'Us,' Smith said, with something that might have been a grin. 'Hold tight,' he added, and then the car was moving fast away from the kerb, rocketing around the corner into the Kirchstrasse, and heading north, while behind them the first flickering flames licked at the doors of the Gestapo *Hauptamt*. The whole thing was over in two minutes – the same two minutes at the end of which Ken Whitehead's carefully-set explosive charges had blown the general administration building at the factory to ruined smithereens.

By the time they reached the bridge across the Mittellandkanal, Harenberg had outdistanced the pursuers. Or else they'd stopped for a moment to see if they could do anything at the factory, Whitehead thought. Whatever the reason, it gave them a much-needed extra minute, and he squinted up at Zittwitz, in the middle of the road, from his perch on the huge concrete stanchion supporting the road bridge across the canal. Although he could not see him, he knew Harenberg was on the other side, matching exactly what Whitehead was doing: grabbing the tripwires of a dozen bundles of stick gelignite, put there earlier by Zittwitz and Baumann. Each was bound by a broad wire band to which was fixed a simple, chemical, trigger detonator, wired in turn to each stick. The trigger was pulled by any pressure applied to a cord with a spring pulley leading to the trigger. Stretch out the cord – as a tripwire, or attached to a door handle – and the moment it was pulled to its fullest extent, it tripped the trigger. He heard Zittwitz's hoarse shout sound in the roadway above. Clambering over the edge of the parapet, Whitehead glanced back down the road.

Coming along, flat out, were two pursuit vehicles led by a motor cycle combination upon whose side-car was mounted a heavy calibre machine-gun.

'Harenberg!' he yelled, and almost before the word had left his mouth, Harenberg was clambering up from below. They ran across the road in opposite directions, Whitehead lashing his tripwire to the rail at Harenberg's side, and Harenberg doing the same on Whitehead's. They could hear the roar of the engines not more than seventy or eighty metres away, as they ran for the waiting pursuit car, which Harenberg had left with its engine ticking over. Clambering aboard, they saw the motor cycle combination sweep around the corner into the straight approaching the bridge, saw the side-car gunner crouching down to swing the barrel of the machine-gun level.

It was almost as if the motor cyclist had been lifted out of the seat by some huge, invisible hand. The tight cord across the road took him across the chest, flipping him backwards as if on a pivot, and then, as Harenberg accelerated into the long curving left turn leading into Lohnde, the bridge disintegrated in a climbing, flame-flecked pillar of exploding masonry and dust. The careening motor cycle, its side-car passenger helpless behind his gun, was tossed into the air like some child's toy, while the lorry immediately behind it had only slightly more than a second to see the gaping hole open up in the roadway under its nose.

The driver's reflexes were very fast, but no power on earth could have stopped the heavy vehicle in the space it had left to it. Wheels locked, stripped tyres laying smoking black rubber tracks on the concrete, the lorry and its screaming load of soldiers went over the edge of the shattered bridge, thundering down the embankment to bump on to its nose, bouncing up high just once. It was in the middle of a cartwheel when its petrol tank exploded, enveloping the truck in flames which were immediately doused as it landed with a gigantic splash in the very centre of the canal, wheels still spinning, and most of the men in it dead before they hit the water.

When they got to the top of the Kirchstrasse, Smith slowed the car, turning left into the Alte Dorfstrasse carefully. On the right hand side, trying to look nonchalant, but plainly relieved that they had arrived, stood Dusty Miller, a haversack swinging from his right hand, his left concealed beneath his coat.

'Goin' anywhere near London?' he said cheerfully to Smith as the car stopped. He climbed in on the far side, pushing the haversack to the floor, and squashing up against Flugge.

'This 'im?' he said, jerking his head at Heineman.

'That's him,' Smith nodded, letting off the handbrake and moving easily into the S-bend at the edge of the town. 'How did everything go?'

'Sweet as a nut,' Miller told him. 'The telephones are all kaput. Some silly sod dropped a grenade down one of the inspection man'oles. Blew every connection in town, shouldn't wonder.' He smiled beatifically at Flugge, who glowered back.

They crossed the Leinebrucke, the Mercedes sinking on its spring as they descended the far side of the humpback. Smith accelerated slightly, heading north and then east to where the Garbsener Landstrasse made its junction with the road they were on.

'What time did you set it for?' he said over his shoulder to Miller.

Dusty looked at his watch, then grinned.

'3.40', he said. 'Any second now.'

Almost as if on cue, they heard the dull sound of the explosion away behind them, back in Seelze. Had they been able to see so far, they would have seen that the pretty little stone Leinebrucke was completely gone, a gaping hole torn right through its old stone arches.

Smith turned left into the Garbsener Landstrasse, and in a moment they were rumbling across the bridge spanning the Mittellandkanal, and entering the outskirts of the town.

'Well,' Smith said, 'that's the easy bit taken care of.'

13

The little village of Schloss Ricklingen stands on a
sloping hill, half a kilometre above the marshy valley of
the Leine, not a great deal more than five kilometres – as
the crow flies – from the centre of Garbsen, and almost
due west of it. It took Smith a little under twenty minutes
to reach the Gasthof Adler which huddles in the lee of
the ruined castle crowning the hump on which
Ricklingen is built. The circular, cobbled street was
empty as the Mercedes rumbled up the slope, and as they
passed the inn, the churchclock on the opposite side of
the street chimed the hour. At the corner, behind the
church, stood a three ton pursuit vehicle with a swivel-
mounted 7.92 Spandau in the rear well, and Flugge's
eyes blazed with triumph as it swung out into the street
and took its place behind them. Smith dashed his hopes
by saying to Miller, 'Is it them ?'

Miller nodded. 'Right on time.'

Now the two vehicles turned sharp right at the
crossroads, taking the road signposted BORDENAU, and
heading past the sports ground on the left, towards the
single, stark, grey building which lay ahead and to their
right.

This was the *Hochhaus,* the concrete blockhouse which
was the Gestapo's maximum security building in the
area. The area for half a hundred metres around it was as

stark as a lunar landscape. There was only one approach road. Nothing could get close to the building without entering an area dominated by a dozen slit windows on each of the seven floors above him. There was no bush, no blade of grass behind which a man could hide – a mouse, even, would have had difficulty in traversing the gravel-strewn surround unseen. Armed guards paced along behind a two foot thick concrete parapet on the roof, from which, on a clear day, they could see the Steinhuder Meer to the west and in the opposite direction, the fuzzy outline of the smoky roofs of Hanover.

Smith drove the car up to the main entrance as if he owned the building personally, not even deigning to notice the SS guard who immediately ran forward from his sentry-box beside the entrance to open the car door.

Smith strode over to the pursuit vehicle, slapping the side of his leg impatiently with the flat of his hand.

'All right, all right, get those skulking dogs out of there!' he snapped. 'Come on, come on, move yourselves!'

Harenberg hastened around to the rear of the truck, letting down the tail-gate as Zittwitz pushed and hustled the six men who had been sitting on the floor of the vehicle to their feet. Harenberg watched coldly as the men, dressed in dirty, ill-fitting, civilian clothes, their mouths firmly taped and gagged, hands tied behind them, and all linked by one rope like circus elephants, stumbled to the ground and stood wide-eyed, as if seeking help from the indifferent SS men standing guard at the entrance.

'Bring them inside!' snapped Smith to Zittwitz. 'You other two, come as well!' Harenberg and Ken Whitehead ran to do his bidding as one of the sentries cranked his telephone and rattled out word that there was an officer outside with six prisoners.

The huge, double, metal doors, steel-clad and without so much as a Judas window or a keyhole on the outside, swung outwards. Inside was a square, concrete ante-chamber with another pair of steel doors on its far side. On the right of the ante-chamber was a glass booth, its greenish-yellow tint betraying the fact that the glass was bullet- and shatter-proof. There was a thin slit at chest level, a two-way microphone/loudspeaker window.

'Your papers,' the *Unterscharführer* at the desk inside said, his face and voice completely devoid of expression. He handed them back without any change in either. 'In order,' he said. He pressed a button and the guards moved to close the outer door, but as they did, Smith exclaimed in impatience and ran back, holding the edge of the door with his hand as he shouted to the men in the waiting Mercedes outside, 'Flugge! You're not coming, too?'

'No,' shouted Miller, his Walther and the nasty jab he'd given Flugge keeping that worthy wisely silent. 'We'll wait here. But be quick, man! It's getting dark, and it's damned cold sitting here!'

'Understood,' Smith grinned, nodding to the guard and letting go of the door. They marched the twin doors closed. Their meeting was marked by a dull, reverberating, metallic boom.

Now, and only now, the *Unterscharführer* in the control box pressed the second button and the inner steel doors swung open. Smith jerked his head, and Whitehead and Zittwitz jabbed their Schmeissers into the backs of the nearest two prisoners, jockeying them into motion and following Smith into the *Empfangshalle,* the reception area of *Hauptamt* VIIB, *Geheime Staats Polizei.*

If painstaking attention to detail can be said to be a kind of genius, then the man who had designed *Hochhaus* 1 for the Gestapo had been a genius. Impregnable from outside attack – its walls were more than four feet thick and built of steel-reinforced concrete – it was also built internally in such a way that, even if anyone succeeded in invading the building, those inside would still command the situation and could, even with the entrance doors breached and the reception hall full of enemy soldiers, effectively hold the *Hochhaus* until either their ammunition ran out or relief arrived.

The building was hexagonal. The rooms occupied by those who worked in it, or those who policed it, were built in seven layered circles around the outside wall of the building. The inner wall, not quite as thick as the outer, was almost circular. There was only one door at each of the seven levels on the inside wall, and each of these was placed in a staggered position so that it could be reached by the wide staircase which mounted the wall in a rising spiral of stone steps, enclosed only by a steel railing and totally exposed on every side. At each of the doorways through which one entered levels one to seven, there was a seven foot long landing made of steel, and the doorways themselves were steel-clad, again without either keyhole or window, except for the tiny spyhole, operated from the inside, which allowed the guard on that level to check whoever wished to enter. No door opened on the outside. The walls were painted a stark and glaring white, and the entire vault was illuminated with harsh lights fixed on the circular balcony which ran the entire way around the inside wall, some fifteen feet above ground. On this balcony there were four guards, constantly vigilant, watching everything that went on below and above.

From the balcony hung down three huge flags : the red, white, and black-striped national flag with its circular swastika emblem in the centre ; the Party banner ; and the death's-head banner of the *Totenkopf* Division of the SS. Beneath the motionless banners was a huge desk flanked by two armed sentries, and behind the desk sat another squat SS *Unterscharführer*.

It was towards this desk that Smith now arrogantly marched at the head of his line of prisoners, his Nazi salute perfunctory and almost bored.

'*Heil Hitler*,' the sergeant said, coming to his feet and snapping out a salute. '*Herr Hauptsturmführer*,' he smiled, staying on his feet. 'You have made quite a *coup*. If I may congratulate the *Haupt* . . . .'

'Yes, yes,' Smith said, waving a dismissive hand. 'Has everything been arranged as I asked ? I want to get back to Hanover tonight !'

'Of course, of course, *Herr Hauptmann*,' the sergeant hastily said. 'As soon as you telephoned. The *Kommandant* made the arrangements himself. Personally.'

'Good,' Smith said, slapping his thigh with his gloves. 'Can we get on, then ?' His tone was imperious, impatient.

'Of course, sir,' the sergeant said. 'But . . . .'

'*But ?*' There was frozen venom in Smith's voice, and he regarded the desk-sergeant as if the man had just eaten a frog.

'The . . . the *Kommandant,* sir. *Obergruppenführer* Kupfer. He wishes to congratulate the *Hauptsturmführer* personally.'

'Oh,' Smith said. Mind racing, he forced himself to smile at the sergeant forgivingly. 'I'm most honoured. But . . . .' He looked around and made a *moue* of distaste. 'Must we wait here?'

'Oh, no, of course not, sir,' the sergeant said, eagerly helpful now that the wicked angry light was no longer in the Gestapo man's eye. 'You will be so kind as to await the *Kommandant* in the Officer's Mess.'

'And the prisoners?'

'We'll have them taken down at the same time, sir,' the sergeant said. 'It's on our way, as you might say.'

'Good,' Smith said. 'You two, come with me.'

The desk sergeant looked up from the telephone when he heard Smith's command, but then he clamped his mouth shut. If that old fool Kupfer was going to tear himself away from his brandy bottle long enough to totter down and congratulate Geis, he must think very highly of him. And if an *Obergruppenführer* SS thought highly of someone, then it wasn't the job of a lowly sergeant to draw that someone's attention to the fact that SS privates, whether on guard duty or whatever, were not allowed in the precincts of the Officer's Mess. The two soldiers probably already knew that, but they, like *Unterscharführer* Greis, knew better than to question the order of their superior. Let Kupfer sort it out himself, Greis thought. It's not my responsibility, anyway. He dialled a number on the phone and spoke briefly. A moment later, the steel door at the foot of the spiral staircase was pushed open by a jackbooted guard armed with a Schmeisser. Whitehead and Zittwitz jabbed the prisoners into movement and they marched across the marble floor, footsteps echoing, and into the concrete corridor. Directly opposite the doorway was an open square area, on the far side of which was a *Personenaufzug,* one of those individual platform lifts running on a continuous belt, so that people working on different levels could step on and off it at any time without having to go through the inner doors constantly, thus reducing security. Next to the *Personenaufzug* was a much bigger lift, with the legend GÜTERAUFZUG printed on a metal plate above the steel concertina doors. Sergeant Greis waved Smith into the lift, standing back as Whitehead and Zittwitz hustled the prisoners past him. If he heard the strangled sounds the prisoners made to attract his attention, if he noticed the rolling eyes they used to try to signal, he gave no sign, and then Smith had pulled the doors across, to the sergeant's farewell call that they would be met below.

The lift sank steadily for what Smith estimated at around twenty-five feet; nothing to be seen through the small window in the lift door but the blank face of a concrete wall sliding upwards. Then the lift jerked to a halt, and Smith pulled back the doors. The simultaneous impressions that the men in the lift received were the whining drone of the air-pumping equipment, the fuggy, warm smell of enclosed humanity, and the uncompromisingly alert hostility of the four SS guards who faced the entrance to the lift with levelled Schmeissers. If the elderly officer in the uniform of an *Obergruppenführer* SS was pleased to see him, Smith thought, he certainly didn't look it.

Outside the *Hochhaus,* Dusty Miller looked at his watch. 4.10. It would be dark in another thirty minutes at the most, maybe even earlier if the greyness continued closing in, the way it was right now. There was an edge on the wind, and he thought he felt the faint flicks of snow in it. With a nod to Jutta Renner, he got out of the car and walked round to the back, stamping his feet and swinging his arms until the sentry, who had looked up at the movement, went back to his own reverie, having to do with a girl named Elsbet, who lived on the Beekestrasse in Ricklingen, and with whom he would be making love three hours from now, when his watch ended. Miller went round to the boot of the Mercedes and opened it. The radio was right where Smith had said it would be, and bending down so that his body shielded what he was doing, he flicked on the switch. The tiny red pilot light glowed, and he let a sigh escape his lips ; the set was all right. He stood up, in one movement bringing down the lid of the boot, and in the other depressing the single red key on the right hand side of the radio transmitter. The boot clunked shut and Dusty stamped his way back to his seat in the car, offering up a silent prayer that Smith's belief that the transmitter was in a position of minimal danger was correct. He had to admit that the reasoning was sound. Even if, in the un-likely event that the signal was picked up, the Gestapo concluded that a transmission was being sent, they would scarcely expect it to be coming from the boot of a staff car parked outside the main entrance to their own headquarters – and at that a staff car with a *Sturmbann-führer* of the SS sitting inside it. Anyway, as Smith had pointed out, with their transmitter literally only fifty feet away from the huge battery of receiving and transmit-ting equipment in the *Hochhaus,* it was extremely unlike-ly that anyone would even notice it. *I just bloody hope so,* Miller thought, looking skywards. *An' I 'ope somebody up there's pickin' it up, or we're all in trouble*. He looked at his watch again. 4.13. They had seventeen minutes, and not a second more.

Wing Commander Dan Johnson had a pal in the American Air Force who'd once delivered himself of a memorable phrase, when asked by Dan to describe how he'd felt the first time he took up a big four-engined plane solo. 'About as nervous,' Mike Dempsey had told him, 'as a long-tailed cat in a roomful of rockin' chairs!' The bizarrely accurate description had stuck in Johnson's mind, and it came to him now as being singularly appropriate to his own situation. For here he was, in the night sky above Germany, in a Heinkel HE-111 twin-engined bomber – U5 FN, he even remembered the registration numbers on the damned thing – which had been forced down over Britain some months earlier. It had landed intact, its crew had been captured, the aircraft itself appropriated by some mysterious branch of the secret service about which, he'd been unceremoniously told, the less he knew the better, and handed back to him at Bovingdon for this special mission.

'Any luck, Taffy?' he shouted to the navigator above the strange broken drone of the engines.

'Not yet, Skipper!' came the reply.

Johnson shook his head. Long-tailed cat my aunt, he thought. Nervous bloody wreck more like it. He knew he really wasn't going to get away with stooging about in Luftwaffe air-space much longer without someone spotting him and requesting identification – it was a miracle no one already had. There was a bloody great Luftwaffe *Jagdgeschwader* at Wunstorf, apart from anything else Jerry might have down there in the murk.

He had to admit, though, that Seelze had been well and truly clobbered. They had flown very low over the area, and Taffy had worked the shutter of the special camera those close-mouthed F.O. types had installed in the plane, getting picture after picture of the devastated laboratories, warehouses, and administration buildings, not to mention the wrecked bridge across the canal. With a huge sigh, he pushed the stick slightly forward and gave the Heinkel some right rudder to bring her round again over Schloss Ricklingen.

'One more time,' he muttered. 'Just one more bloody time.'

'*Herr Kommandant!*' smiled Smith, stepping forward with his hand out, brushing past the armed guards. 'How kind of you to take such trouble.'

'With such an accomplishment, it is the least I could do,' the old man said, the austere look making way for a weak smile. 'You may send your men back. The prisoners will be taken to the detention cells by my guards.'

'Of course,' Smith said, standing away as the guards fell into formation behind the six mutely beseeching prisoners, still trying desperately to make some sound behind the gags which would communicate their real identity to the *Kommandant* or one of the SS guards.

'You men wait for me upstairs,' he told Whitehead and Zittwitz. Both nodded and saluted, and almost as an afterthought, Smith stopped the former, lifting the satchel off the big man's arm. 'A moment,' he said, apologetically, to the *Kommandant*.

'Of course,' the old man said, cursing the damned Gestapo agent for being so long-winded. It was chilly and uncomfortable down here in the bunker, and he'd have much preferred to be back in his own warm office, sipping cognac and day-dreaming of the good years in the army before these Nazi thugs had taken everything over.

Smith lifted a flat package out of the satchel, and then with an almost imperceptible nod to Whitehead, handed it back.

'I should be about ten minutes,' he said affably to Whitehead. 'Not much longer.'

'*Jawohl, Herr Hauptmann,*' Whitehead said, clicking his heels. Message sent, received, understood : in about ten minutes, Smith would be coming into the *Empfangshalle* upstairs and they'd better be ready. He nodded to himself : they would.

'With your permission, *Herr Obergruppenführer,* I'll see that these men are, ah, properly accommodated.' A silky smile touched Smith's lips, and the old man gave a short nod. 'I'll wait in the mess,' he said. Damned if I'm going to have any of that Gestapo business, he thought, letting nothing show on his face. Let the man have his gloating moment of triumph, if he needed it – and most of them seemed to. All that was expected of him, Kupfer, was that he would give Geis a pat on the head, a drink – strange how all these Gestapo monsters loved praise from a professional soldier ! – and forget the whole thing. He walked away down a corridor to the right of the one along which the group was proceeding, while Smith followed the phalanx straight ahead to another solid steel door, outside which stood an armed guard. He came to attention, saluted, and worked a lever which opened the door. The guards hustled the six prisoners inside and lined them up in front of a pudgy-faced, middle-aged man wearing rimless spectacles and the uniform of an *Untersturmführer* SS .

'I am Geis,' Smith snapped. 'These are the British saboteurs I have taken prisoner.'

'We're getting quite a lot of those these days,' smiled the desk-soldier, ingratiatingly. 'What with the other three . . . .'

'Yes, yes,' Smith rasped. 'Where are they?'

The man's eyes widened. 'You wish to see them?'

'If it would not be too much trouble,' Smith said, sarcasm hardening his tone.

'Of course, if the *Herr Hauptmann* insists . . . ?' the SS man stammered.

'Get on with it, man!' Smith said, irritably. 'We haven't all day!'

'Cell Four,' the SS man nodded, jerking a thumb over his shoulder. Behind him, Smith could see through the barred glass window in the upper half of the door. There was a corridor on the right hand side of which were four barred doors.

'First,' the second lieutenant said, 'let's see what these beauties have to say for themselves.'

'Leave that!' snapped Smith, as the SS man reached for the strip of cloth holding the gag in place in the mouth of the real Gestapo man, Geis. Geis's eyes rolled upward in entreaty, and he made muffled sounds of near-pain as he tried facially to communicate the fact that he wanted the gag ripped away, that Smith was a British agent, and that all Geis's fellow-prisoners were soldiers of the Third Reich. It was an impossible task, and anyway, the second lieutenant had already turned back to face Smith, his face forming a look of protesting surprise.

'But it is normal procedure . . . ' he began.

'My dear *Untersturmführer,*' Smith said silkily. 'Do I assume you wish to instruct me in correct procedure?'

The man looked at Smith, his words tailing into an audible gulp at the size of his *gaffe.* He shook his head inarticulately, anxiously.

'Very well,' Smith said. 'The cells, I think. You have space?'

'Cells two and three, sir,' the desk-soldier managed. 'They have been prepared.'

'Good, good,' Smith replied absently. 'Open, please.'

He snapped his fingers, and the SS man hurried around his desk, reaching into his pocket for a key with which he unlocked a steel drawer set into the wall. He slid it out, and from it took three more keys. Smith could see that there was a separate slot for each key in the drawer. The SS man came anxiously back around his desk and opened the corridor door with a flourish, nodding to Smith to precede him into the corridor. He was anxious to curry favour now, for this unsmiling bastard obviously enjoyed his rank and even more obviously had the ear of General Kupfer. *Untersturmführer* Gustav Stuckrath didn't want any black marks on his dossier, thank you, especially not if they were signed by a *Hauptsturmführer Gestapo.*

Now he went ahead to open the cells numbered three and two. He turned to face Smith with a smile, as though expecting praise. Smith ignored him, motioning to the guards to move. They hustled Chevalier, Geis and one of the other prisoners into Cell 3, the other trio into Cell 2. Then they came out and stood, eyes fixed on infinity, awaiting Smith's orders like the fawning Stuckrath.

'Shall I lock the cells, *Herr Hauptmann?*' he asked.

'Give me the keys,' Smith said, extending a hand.

Stuckrath's eyebrows climbed, but this time he held his tongue and handed over the keys. He felt a little self-satisfaction at what had happened, for now when he wrote his report he would point out that the Gestapo man had quite definitely and quite deliberately exceeded his authority. He'd do it subtly, of course, but he'd fix this hard-eyed swine's wagon all right.

Even as the thought faded, Stuckrath died.

Somewhere in the edges of his peripheral vision, he probably saw the gun in Smith's hand. Somewhere on the far reaches of his vocal chords a scream might have been quickening. It never left his throat. The silenced Walther in Smith's hand coughed and the second-lieutenant was hurled backwards by the force of the bullet, smashing against the four astonished guards, jamming them together in the narrow corridor as they fought to bring their own weapons into use. But the machine-pistols were clumsy and they were off-balance and confused. Smith's face was completely without pity. He shot the four men down as ruthlessly and efficiently as if he had been clipping the bowls off clay pipes in a fairground booth, one-two-three-four, the corridor reeking of cordite and wisping gunsmoke as the last of the SS guards slid to the floor, legs kicking convulsively as his Schmeisser clattered harshly on the concrete.

Even as the guard fell, Smith was moving, jamming the key into the lock and swinging wide the door of Cell Four.

The foetid smell that belched in his face was revolting, the disgusting stench of a cess-pit. He went in, fighting down the desire to retch. It was hard to see, but his eyes adjusted to the gloom and he saw them then and could control his stomach no more.

There were three of them. Their bodies were naked and blood-spattered, covered in black bruises and smaller spots that might have been burns. They hung by emaciated arms from iron rings let into the walls four feet above Smith's head. All three had obviously been brutally, mercilessly tortured. All three were just this side of death.

Smith went closer to the awful things on the wall.

'Franklin?' he said. Then he repeated the name, louder, with the authority – of a command. 'Allison? Smith?'

'Here', one of them said. He moved his head painfully. Beneath the matted beard the chewed lips tried to shape words. There was no life in the swollen eyes.

'I'm British!' Smith said. 'British!'

'Yeh,' the man said. His head lolled.

Smith went closer to the second man, the one in the centre. The cruelties the prisoner had suffered were written on his body in blood, and his face was puffed and swollen, the eyes tiny spots of dull shine behind broken cheekbones.

'Michael?' Smith whispered. 'Michael?'

The dull light hidden in the bulging folds of battered flesh brightened a fraction. The prisoner tried to lift his head, but could not do it. A tear rolled down the scarred face.

'Day?' he managed. 'Day?'

Smith's hand, strangely gentle, touched the broken face.

'Yes,' he said softly. 'It's me.'

He looked at his watch. It was 4.21.

Wing Commander Dan Johnson, DSO, wheeled the lumbering Heinkel around in a tight turn, homing in on the bearing Taff had given him. They had picked up the beam from down below about six minutes before, and Taff had plotted it as Johnson made his sweeping circle over the relatively empty countryside south of the Otternhagener Moor and came back on to 238. Now he pushed the nose of the bomber down into the murky, low-lying cloud, holding her tightly as she bucketed in the air-pockets going in, while Taffy scrambled to the bomb-aimer's position in the nose of the plane. Normally, an HE-111 would have had a crew of five, but they'd been told they'd have to fly her the best way they could, since they'd need all the space they had for the return flight. The boffins had rigged special controls so that Johnson could operate everything from the pilot's seat, and what little he couldn't manage Taffy handled. It had worked fine so far, but the real test was going to be now, as they came roaring in on bearing 238. They broke out of the belly of the cloud-base and saw the open, wooded countryside below them, patches of evening mist seeping up from the river bottoms like ghosts stealing land. Then the wide, white ribbon of the Bremen road slid beneath their path and Johnson steepened the dive, pushing the throttles to full power. The fuselage trembled as the engines gave their unbridled bellow, and the Heinkel sped even faster in its downward trajectory – down and down and down until Johnson was holding her at just above 200 feet. Then he levelled off over the top of the pines on the hump of the Rettmerberg, the nose of the plane pointing straight at the ugly, grey block of the target half a mile ahead, its tall radio mast like some spidery finger reaching into the overcast as if trying to touch them. Taffy's voice crackled in the pilot's ear.

'Lovely, Skipper, lovely, lovely, hold her there, lovely, lovely, bombs *gone* !'

Johnson felt the plane lift as the first stick soared downwards from her belly, and he took her over in a tight right-hand turn, the Leine glinting below as he pulled around for the second run and Taffy's well-aimed straddle walked in thundering, smashing eruptions of exploding earth across the empty ground on the northern side of the *Hochhaus,* and finally burst in fury against the faceless walls of the building itself. Johnson glanced at his watch and grinned. It was exactly 4.30.

Smith closed the door of Cell Four and locked it, his face like stone. He had tried, no matter under what provocation, to avoid hate. Hate was a cancer to destroy any man who succumbed to it, a poison to warp any mind it entered. Until he had come here he had not hated the Nazis. There was a war, of course, and in a war it was his duty to kill Nazis. But that was a cerebral decision. If the Nazis won the war, the world would be enslaved. Smith believed in freedom – for himself, for every man – and knew that Britain's cause was right and just. He did not hate Germany or her people, he had told himself. Until now.

Now he stood outside Cell Four and the hate blazed inside him with a terrible ferocity that was the worse for not being able to release it in a screaming shout of anger, defiance, revenge. Somewhere in the back of his mind a deep, dark, red throbbing thing was growing and growing, throbbing and growing and driving him deeper and deeper into the hatred rising in him. That he had done what he had to do inside the Cell was no longer of importance. That one of the broken things had been his younger brother mattered no more either. What mattered now was revenge and his mind was consumed by a need for it.

He kicked aside the door of Cell Three and went in. Bending over Chevalier he ripped the gag away from the man's mouth.

'Don't bother calling for help, Ritter,' he ground out, as the man worked his dry, crushed tongue around in his numbed mouth. 'You know where you are – so you ought to know how much good it will do you.'

'This ... what it ... was for?' croaked Paul Ritter. 'This?'

Smith nodded. 'Franklin, Allison and Smith,' he said. 'You betrayed all three of them to the Gestapo, didn't you? You knew what would happen to them, didn't you? Didn't you?' His big hand shook the bound Ritter violently and Ritter's mouth formed a smile like a razor cut.

'Do . . . it . . . you . . . ,' he panted. 'Yet.'

Smith's smile was colder than Ritter's, and he did not speak. Pulling a roll of wide sticking tape from his pocket, he stripped a piece off. Then he took the flat package which Whitehead had handed to him earlier and with the tape he bound it to the side of Ritter's head. The man's eyes widened as Smith worked, and he shook his head violently to try to dislodge the package, but to no avail. Now Smith dragged the Gestapo man, Geis, across the cell by the leg. He jammed him back to back with Ritter and lashed their arms together with the remainder of the sticking plaster.

'I was going to use that,' Smith said, nodding at the

flat package, 'in the lift-shaft. Until I saw what had been done to our people.'

'Is ... was it ... any worse ... than this?' Ritter managed.

'I don't know,' Smith said. 'And I don't care.' He bent down and put the gag back into Ritter's mouth, tying the binder tightly behind his head.

'Goodbye, Ritter,' Smith said tonelessly. 'Listen to that for the last ten minutes of your worthless life.'

Without looking at them again, he got up and went out of the cell, locking it behind him. Then he locked the corridor door and put the keys neatly back on the desk of the dead *Untersturmführer*. The outer office was quietly peaceful, no hint of the bloody mess behind the corridor door impinging on its green and cream tranquillity. Smith caught a glimpse of a wild-eyed, white-faced man in the mirror on the far wall, and for a moment did not recognize himself. Then he rapped on the steel door with the barrel of one of the machine-pistols he had picked up.

The guard outside worked the lever, and Smith went outside, nodding to the man, who saluted. Inside Cell 3, Ritter heard the door open and he tried very, very hard to shout for help or make some noise that the guard might hear. Smith had done his job far too well for that, and the most Ritter managed was a strangled croak that he knew would not have carried ten feet. He slumped back against the panting Geis, feeling the sweat breaking from his skin, shaking his head to try loosening the bindings holding the flat package Smith had put there. It was no use. He slumped back, exhausted, fear pouring into every crevice of his brain as water submerges a cabbage heart, conscious only now of the sound at the side

147

of his head, a sound that seemed to grow steadily
louder.

Tick tick tick tick tick.

The sudden, total unexpectedness of the bombs falling on
the building created a complete panic inside the *Hochhaus*.
Even though everyone in it had been assured, time and
again, that the building was virtually bombproof, that was
not quite the same as being in the building when it was
being bombed, Women clerks and soldiers with no tunics,
old and young all ran into the corridors on every level.
Women were running screaming from the offices on the
northern side of the fourth level, where the effect of the
first bombs had been most strongly felt. The guards on
the balcony above the *Empfangshalle* came clattering
down the curving stone staircase to congregate around
the central desk, where Sergeant Greis was frantically
trying to contact *Zentrale* for instructions, not realizing
that everyone else in the *Hochhaus* was trying to do
exactly the same thing, jamming the switchboard completely. The guards were all grouped around the desk,
waving their arms towards the upper floors and
shouting angrily, when Whitehead and Zittwitz calmly
lifted their Schmeissers and made a curving run towards
the double doors leading towards the corridor in which
the lift shafts were situated, firing in scything bursts as
they went. The first bullets slammed the startled sentries
off their feet before they could even react, and then the
next bursts sprayed into the bunched soldiers around
Greis, who were whirling around, lifting their machine-
pistols in belated reaction to the shocking suddenness of
their comrades' deaths. The men went down in bloody
tatters, bodies hurled sliding in smeared ugly streaks of

blood on the heedless marble, torn to pieces by the hurricane of heavy calibre lead. Sergeant Greis, with four neat holes stitched across the front of his uniform jacket, was the last to go down, snatching at the banner of the *Totenkopf* as he fell, and bringing it down upon his twitching body like a shroud. Even as the death's-head flag settled on Greis's porcine form, Zittwitz and Whitehead were beside the double steel doors, and Whitehead ripped away the tab of the chemical fuse protruding from beneath the heavy lip of the overlap. When they had gone through the doors earlier, Whitehead had surreptitiously slapped a thick strip of plastic explosive, ready palmed in his hand, into the overlap, a two-inch strip of heavy steel bar which concealed the door join. Compressed behind this bar, the explosion generated enormous power, splitting the locking mechanism apart as easily as if it had been the door of a doll's house. Almost before the thunder of the explosion had receded, Whitehead and Zittwitz were in movement from their protected positions against the heavy wall each side of the door, wrenching the doors open wide, and emptying their Schmeissers into the bodies of the three guards who had come running towards the source of the explosion and stood now framed in the smoking entrance way. Pausing only to snatch up the machine-pistols of the fallen men, Zittwitz and Whitehead pounded over to the lift shafts, Zittwitz covering as Whitehead knelt in front of the *Personenaufzug* and ripped open the haversack. Moving fast, he took out grenades with stop-watch-setting mechanisms, slapping them on the floor of each platform as it went by him, the first set at three minutes, the next 2:30, and so on, his nimble fingers making short work of the task.

As he slapped down the last grenade, set for 90 seconds, the building shook again as the bomber overhead made its second and final run, machine-guns chattering this time, and the stick of bombs right on target. They smashed into the northern side of the building, this time cracking the wall of the *Hochhaus* and causing a slight subsidence of the floor on the seventh level. Slight though it was, added to the total un-expectedness of the attack, it created a panic among the senior officers whose offices were situated there. They came out into the corridors, heading towards the lifts in a barely controlled running rout, and bunching into the open space before the doors in exactly the same moment that Whitehead's grenade reached the seventh floor and exploded. This wicked blast filled the air with whickering chunks of shrapnel, cutting a wide swathe through the ranks of the scrabbling soldiers, killing the three nearest the *Personenaufzug* instantly, and smashing seven others in tattered moaning heaps to the suddenly bloody floor. The entire corridor was filled with chok-ing smoke and coughing, cursing, broken bodies of men moaning for help. Their very appearance created more panic in those who were just arriving on the scene, heightened in turn by the chain explosion of Whitehead's other grenades as they tore different levels of the lift shaft to smithereens, starting tentative tongues of fire on the third and sixth levels, which fell back and then surged again, taking hold, filling the corridors with smoke and tongues of fire, driving back towards the dangers they had just fled the people who had instinc-tively run for the lift shafts, trapping them in agonized indecision. Their only solution was the single metal doors which led out on to the inner circular stairway –

that, at least, would lead them to safety.

So they stumbled and fought their way round the circular corridors, possessed now only of blind panic, self-preservation their only instinct. Screams of agonized pain echoed through the faceless corridors as people were heedlessly trampled underfoot by the surging mob, no longer some hundreds of frightened individuals on each level, but a series of mindless savage animals.

Smith got as far as the passageway down which *Obergruppenführer* Klaus Kupfer had earlier disappeared towards the Officer's Mess before the alarm klaxon erupted into deafening action like the last call for the boat to Hell.

Men came boiling into the corridors all around them, struggling into uniform jackets and steel helmets. A big sergeant was shouting at them to follow him.

'You!' the sergeant shouted behind Smith. 'Hey, you!'

Smith kept going, hurrying towards the lift shaft not more than a dozen yards ahead of them in the narrow corridor.

'*You!*' shouted the sergeant. '*Stop! Stop that man!*'

He had turned now and was running towards them, and, as he did, the other soldiers in the corridor were turning, following instinctively as the sergeant shouted orders.

Smith's face went hard and empty and the boiling hate erupted. Turning, he emptied the Schmeisser into the ranks of the soldiers running at him. It was a terrible, awful sight : he was putting heavy calibre bullets moving at well over 700 miles an hour into the bodies of men not six feet away at the rate of around five hundred a minute, and the things that happened when he pulled the trigger were dreadful to see. Men were smashed off their feet as if by some giant, invisible, club, and the walls and floor of the corridor were turned instantly into something more like an abattoir. The stink of scorched clothing, the sweet, cloying, reek of blood, mixed with the acrid tang of cordite and burned powder, hung in the swaying smoke as the scrabbling, screaming soldiers fell backwards in total panic, away from the terrifying figure of the huge man with the gargoyle face as empty of expression as the face of the Reaper himself, who was using the blazing machine-gun as if it were a blowtorch and he clearing cobwebs.

Then Smith threw the empty, red-hot gun at the dim, bunched figures he could see through the curtain of smoke, and leaped back into the lift, slamming the doors over and jabbing the button. In its own infuriatingly deliberate manner the lift jerked into action, and Smith looked at his watch, panting, his face speckled with pinhead powderburns.

Damn, damn, damn!

As the lift came up to ground level, Zittwitz threw open the gates. Before Smith was quite out, Zittwitz was already slamming shut the lift gates, but before he did so, he rolled a stop-timed grenade into the lift cage. As the door contact was made, the lift began to sink in response to the signals from the soldiers below, who were pressing the call button to bring it down. As the lift sank, Zittwitz was already sliding on his knees into the open hallway, where he could see Smith and Whitehead spraying bullets upwards, the shots smacking great chunks of plaster off the walls around the steel doorways, driving the people trying to get out of the smoking corridors back against those behind them. A man screamed and went over the edge of the rail on the fourth level, the pressure of those behind him irresistible, forcing him to his death. Zittwitz added his fire-power to that of the other two, moving towards the double doors leading into the concrete antechamber where their papers had been inspected.

Smith was already there, swinging back the huge steel doors and blasting down the sentries inside without giving them so much as a chance, while Whitehead ran at the bullet-proof glass booth. He slid something flat through the slit and the *Unterscharführer* inside looked at it, then at Whitehead, his mouth dropping open and his eyes bulging.

'Cheerio,' Whitehead said, and hit the floor as the explosion made a dull, flat, contained sound inside the booth, and the berserk, scrabbling figure of the German disappeared, while something slick and messy slid down the opaquely splintered glass.

Whitehead was the last out. As he came through the doors, he had time only to descry the sprawled form of a sentry slumped outside his box beside the door. Smith was already in the driving seat of the Mercedes and moving it away as Whitehead ran for the three-tonner, which Harenberg was wheeling after Smith.

'*Alles in Ordnung?*' shouted Miller, as Smith let in the clutch fast, jamming down the accelerator. The big man didn't answer, giving his entire attention to correcting the fishtailing swerve the big car made as the wheels screamed and spun on the gravel of the empty surround. Then with a surge of power the Mercedes was moving, and Smith slapped down the light switch, the powerful beams slicing ahead of them into the dark murk, revealing the empty road ahead. Like two pursued animals, the low-slung car and the lumbering pursuit vehicle sped across the open ground, and as they reached the road, Smith threw the wheel to the left, dry-skidding the vehicle so that he was already gaining forward momentum before the Mercedes was quite finished sliding to the right. They roared into the left-hand arm of the fork and he pushed the accelerator down to the floor, turning his head towards the *Hochhaus*.

Almost as if his movement had been a signal, the last of the phosphorus grenades, which Whitehead had slung, satchel and all, into the communications *Zentrale* on the ground level, went off with a sizzling boom, their stunning white glare flickering against the grey underbelly of the lowering snow-clouds like lightning. Even above the whistling roar of the car they could hear the rumble of collapsing masonry, and Miller whistled through his teeth.

'4.35,' Smith said, satisfaction in his voice. '*Alles in Ordnung!*'

If he remembered that the bomb taped to Ritter had also been set for 4.35, he did not mention it. He checked the mirror. The three-tonner was bundling along on their tail and behind it the road was black and empty.

'Good job you're not in England, Skipper,' Miller told him.

'What?' Smith was concentrating on the road, empty and straight all the way into Bordenau.

'I said, good job you wasn't in England,' Miller repeated. 'Get five years for that, you can.'

It was no good, Smith thought, he was hooked. He

had to know the answer.

'Five years for what?' he asked.

'Riotously Demolishing a Hovel,' Miller told him.

14

They eased quietly through Bordenau, its streets devoid
of traffic, all but a few late shoppers at home behind the
neatly drawn curtains that gave off faint squares of light
up the side streets behind the church. Now they turned
left, taking the road across the sharply bending
bridgeway over the Leine, with the dark hulk of the
boat-shed on their right, brightly lit on the river side.
Smith pulled the Mercedes to one side, waving
Harenberg past in the three-tonner, and then drove the
car to the centre of the smaller, stone, hump-backed
bridge which crossed the narrow lake on the west of the
marshy meadow through which the river meandered.
This stretch of water, perhaps sixty metres wide and
stretching several hundred metres south alongside the
road between Poggenhagen and Wunstorf, had no
name; it was just a run-off from the Leine.

Getting out of the car, Smith took a haversack from
the boot and out of it pulled a coil of thin, strong copper
wire. This he gave to Miller.

'I want you to rig wires to anything in the car that will
move if the car is moved – forward, backwards, upwards, sideways. Anything. And then I want the other
end of those wires rigged to – this!'

He plunged his fist into the haversack and came out
with a bundle of stick gelignite such as the ones which
had been used to blow the bridges at Seelze. 'Get

weaving,' he said. 'We haven't got much time. Dr Heineman, Dr Gessler, you will be kind enough to get out of the car!'

The two scientists obeyed immediately. What they had witnessed today had convinced them that this cold-eyed *Engländer* was a man who could do any damned thing he said he could do. If he'd told them to start flying towards England at that moment, they would have probably started flapping their arms and given it a try. Jutta Renner got out behind the two men, the pistol she had held on them the whole time since they had left Seelze still in her hand.

'Take them over to the truck,' Smith told her, and the girl nodded, prodding the two men into a stumbling trot as Smith laid a detaining hand on the shoulder of *Sturmbannführer* Flugge, who had also half risen in anticipation of being told to get out.

'No, no, my dear Klaus,' Smith said, pushing the man firmly back into his seat. 'Not you. You're staying here.' He turned his head. 'Dusty?'

'Ten seconds,' Miller's disembodied voice called from beneath the car.

'Ken?' Smith said, handing the big man the explosives.

'Got you,' Whitehead said.

He bent down and said something to Miller, and then came up erect, four strands of wire in his hand. These he twisted together and then bound very tightly to the trip-trigger of the gelignite. The sound of the tiny ratchet as he set the fuse for instantaneous was very loud in the still night. Then he bent down and leaned over Flugge.

'Legs apart, please.'

Flugge looked at him with his mouth agape, obeying

without thinking, and then surging up, as if to struggle, when Whitehead slapped the bundle of explosive between his legs on the car seat. Smith's pistol-muzzle at his temple made the Nazi sink back, his eyes wild.

'You can't do this, you can't mean to do this,' he spluttered. 'This is nothing short of cold-blooded murder!'

'I'd expect you to know about that,' Smith said. 'So I'll accept your word it is.'

Smith now ran a length of line round Flugge's tightly bound legs to the stanchion of the bridge, and then back to the steering column of the car, winding it around and finally breaking it off.

'Now don't you even hiccup,' he said to Flugge. 'Or you'll be spread all over *Landkreis* Neustadt.'

'This is monstrous!' *Sturmbannführer* Flugge snapped. 'You give me no chance of survival. One movement....'

'You'd better make sure you tell anyone who comes along not to move you – or anything else,' Smith told him coldly. 'And you'd better pray it isn't someone who has a reason for disliking Nazis in general or you in particular!'

'I appeal to you,' Flugge begged. 'As one officer to another. This is not war. Gentlemen do not fight like this!'

'You don't appeal to me one bit, you snake-eyed bastard!' Smith snapped. 'If it wasn't for the fact that you're more useful to us this way, I'd have taken great pleasure in shooting you personally – a long time ago!'

He waved the other two on ahead, and they trotted down the slight incline of the bridge to where the truck stood waiting, engine idling. Harenberg was leaning out of the driving cab looking for them. They climbed aboard and the truck moved off into the darkness, stopping at the junction of the main road between Wunstorf and Poggenhagen. The tail lights blinked once and then they were gone, leaving the night silent again except for the occasional croak of a marsh bird somewhere along the reedy banks of the Leine and the steady, monotonous, string of oaths coming from the slavering lips of *Sturmbannführer* Klaus Flugge in the booby-trapped car on the bridge.

'Only seventeen hours ?' Miller asked, incredulously. 'We've only been here seventeen hours ?' Whitehead nodded.

They were at their final rendezvous, outside a small training aerodrome which lay about a kilometre from the western edge of the little village of Poggenhagen, and not much more than six south of the spot on which they had made their landing the night before, on the chilly wastes of the Totes Moor. The night was solid black now, with an edge of snow in the air. Despite the heavy German greatcoats, there wasn't a man in the truck who wasn't shivering.

Smith had parked the truck, without lights, on the side of the road opposite the edge of the woods, which came almost to the fringe of the cleared spaces in which the barrack huts stood. *Am Flugplatz,* as the aerodrome had been called before the war, was now a training field for Lutwaffe pilots, a simple landing and take-off ground with an A-shaped set of runways, a small control tower close to the apex of the A at the northern end of the longest runway. There was a drop-pole barrier across the entrance road, with the usual diagonally striped sentry-box and a Luftwaffe corporal guarding it.

Their preparations were all made; all that remained now was for Dusty Miller to do the work that only he could do. Smith touched his shoulder and pointed at the airfield with his chin. Miller nodded, and the two of them swung to the ground, Miller melting into the darkness like a wraith, as Smith walked across the road towards the sentry, who was stamping his numb feet on the concrete, blowing into his mittened hands.

'By God,' he said, as Smith came near. 'It's going to snow. I can smell it.'

'I think you're right,' Smith said. 'Listen, am I on the right road to get to Klein Heidorn?'

'Yes, you're right,' the sentry told him. 'But it's a bit complicated. Got your map?'

Smith fumbled in his pocket and brought out the map, and the sentry bent over it, his woollen-clad finger stabbing down as he gave Smith instructions, and Dusty Miller slid past in the shadows behind the sentry-box moving unerringly out towards the middle of the airfield, fading from sight.

'Well, thanks a lot,' Smith said, 'that's very helpful.'

'Nothing to say thanks for,' the sentry replied. 'Have a beer for me in the *Blaue Hecht*.' He turned to go into the sentry-box and Smith who had half-turned away, was around like a panther, an arm like a bar of steel clamping across the man's throat and choking off any sound he might have made, while an inexorable pressure on the carotid artery rendered him unconscious within twenty seconds. Smith dragged the man into the shadows, and then lifted the drop-pole to the vertical position. He flicked on his torch once, twice, and Harenberg gave him an answering flash with the masked headlights. Smith heard the engine start up and

Harenberg swung the three-tonner across the road and past the entrance, halting as Smith dropped the pole behind the truck, and then swung aboard. Harenberg eased the truck into gear. They trickled slowly along the feeder road in front of the two-storeyed control tower. Its windows were still illuminated and they could see people moving around inside.

'Hold it!' Smith hissed, leaning around the side of the cab so that Harenberg could hear him. With a slight squeal of brakes that sounded like the clap of doom to the tense men, the truck eased to a stop. As it did, they heard for the first time the deep, throaty sound of an approaching plane, the burrr-vvmmmm-burrrvvmmmm of its engines.

'That's a Jerry,' Whitehead said.

'No it's not,' Smith told him. He sat down on the metal seat of the big Spandau machine gun, and swivelled it around until he had the barrel aimed squarely at the big lighted windows of the control tower. Then, at the same moment, the night was split open: all along the wide concrete runway ahead of the truck, as Dusty Miller joined up the connections in his manhole at the centre of the grass runway fringe, the landing lights flicked into life, casting an almost shockingly bright light over the entire airfield area, bathing the truck in a halo of illumination. And at exactly the same instant Smith pressed the firing button of the big Spandau.

'There they are!' Taffy yelled, and Wing Commander Dan Johnson saw the bright rows of the landing lights standing out in the darkness down below like disembodied Christmas-tree illuminations. He banked sharply, dropping the Heinkel into a side-slip that brought him over the sprinkled houses of Poggenhagen and into a tight curving approach from the south towards the runway he could see so brightly lit ahead of him. He had to hand it to Smith and his boys. 17.00 hours, they'd said. And right on the button the lights had come on. Then he cleared his mind for the final approach, concentrating on getting the unfamiliar bomber on to the centre line, eyes moving automatically from altimeter to level indicator to air-speed indicator, feeling for the moment, that seat-of-the-pants instinctively known moment, when it would be safe to let her drop. He made his decision and there was a weightless second as the plane bellied down to become earthbound again, the wheels kissing the tarmac with a singing squeal as he slowed her down, reversing pitch and braking in a roar of noise that coincided with an astonishing explosion which ripped the top of the control tower off as if it had been a packet of cereal, sending a huge orange-yellow fireball of flame climbing sixty feet into the air. He saw the truck swerving out on to the tarmac towards the plane, and started to turn the Heinkel round.

Smith's first blasting volley with the Spandau shattered every window on the upper storey of the control tower as he wheeled the big gun in a tight arc, forward and then back, walking the barrel the whole length of the building. There were shouts of astonished surprise, audible faintly above the screams of dying men, and then the siren surged into life, rising into a crescendo of sound, high-pitched and constant, that brought men tumbling out of the barrack huts on the other side of the airfield.

Smith swung the Spandau around as Whitehead emerged from the driving cab, running crouched towards the control tower building. There was a squat green transformer just to the right of the building, and Whitehead ran into the space between the two. His right arm arched, lobbing two grenades into the broken window-frames up above. Turning, he ripped the pin from another, and jammed it into one of the vents of the transformer, turning to run towards the truck as the first spiteful return fire began to come from the approaching men. Then the grenades blew, taking the top off the control tower, raining bricks and wood and shards of glass on those below. Harenberg had already put the truck into motion, and Smith opened up again with the big Spandau. The line of running men melted to the ground like wheat before the cutting edge of reaper blades. There were hoarse shouts of panic, and somewhere a man was screaming in a high shrill threnody of pain.

Whitehead ran in a curving tangent to meet the moving truck as it lumbered now towards the waiting Heinkel. He jumped on to the running board and hung on there as they moved down the runway, piling out when Harenberg jammed on the brakes and gave a shout to Smith, who fired one last burst which emptied the Spandau and then jumped over the side of the truck, running towards the plane as Harenberg put the truck into gear. The big three-tonner lurched away out of control across the runway, bumping over the grassy space and eventually smashing a wooden hut to tinder before it came to a stop, motor still racing, against a tree at the edge of the woods. By the time it did, Miller – who had been the first aboard – had already dragged Whitehead in by main force. They lay sprawled on the floor of the plane, panting from the exertion, the tension, the pain. Johnson gunned the motors into full, surging life, and the Heinkel started rolling up the runway. With his hand locked on Whitehead's wrist, and Whitehead's on his own, Smith swung upwards towards the narrow door, and then he was aboard.

Behind them on the runway, squads of men were kneeling now to fire rifles and machine-pistols after the moving plane, and they could clearly hear the bullets ripping into the fuselage and wing surfaces.

'Damn this for a lark!' Whitehead snapped, clambering into the rear gun turret up behind the pilot of the Heinkel. Almost petulantly he slapped the breech open, checked the ammunition, slammed it shut, cocked the weapon, and opened fire.

The motor cycle combination with the machine-gun side-car was within fifty yards of the plane when Whitehead's burst hit it. He had not been aware, until he pressed the firing button, that the guns were loaded with tracer, but now he saw the fiery missile soar towards its mark, smash through the driver's knee and explode the petrol tank with a stunningly sudden flash of flame that blew the bike apart and threw the tattered burning things which had been riding it twenty feet into the air. Whitehead raked the tarmac behind them as the plane picked up speed, grinning with delight as he saw he could skip the tracers off the solid concrete surface like a kid playing ducks and drakes. Then he felt the soft sag that meant the plane was off the ground, and he lifted his thumb off the button.

In the belly of the plane, Smith was standing up to speak to the pilot as Ken Whitehead clambered up out of the gun turret. He grinned at Whitehead, gave a thumbs up sign, and banged Johnson on the arm.

'Home, James!' he said, his battered face alight with good humour.

'You bet your bloody life!' yelled back the airman. 'You bet your bloody life.'

15

The Prime Minister watched without speaking as the Chairman walked to the door with Smith, his hand on the big man's shoulder. The Marine guard opened the door, the two men shook hands. Smith smiled at something the Chairman said, his ugly face boyish and rested. The de-briefings were over, the reports were filed, the dossiers were closed. He went out without looking back.

The Chairman nodded to the Marine sergeant, who quietly closed the doors as the NSA chief walked back across the Cabinet Room towards the Prime Minister's seat. He pulled over a chair and sat down, arms folded on the black-out material stretched over the trestle table.

'Well, Prime Minister,' he said. 'They did it.'

'They did,' Churchill agreed. 'Damned if I know how.'

'A little something to celebrate, perhaps?'

'Why not?' Churchill nodded. 'You didn't tell him?'

'He doesn't need to know.'

'They did a fine job anyway,' Churchill said.

'Well, they would have,' the Chairman replied. 'Every man on that team was a hand-picked mayhem artist. Gangsters, assassins, bomb-experts, garrotters, knife-fighters – savages, every one of them. Where Smith finds out about them I don't know. And I'm not sure I want to know,' he added.

'Smith's savages,' Churchill mused.

'It certainly describes them.' The Chairman placed the two glasses on the table. The Prime Minister picked up his balloon and swirled the amber liquid around under his nose.

'So,' he said. 'Smith – and his people – believe that their mission was accomplished as planned ?'

'They do, sir. And it was. Smith's job was to expose Chevalier, or rather Ritter. He did so. His job was to attack and destroy the laboratory of Reidel and de Haen at Seelze, and to kidnap Heineman. He did that. It was at his own request that I allowed him to take on the additional job of getting into the Gestapo headquarters at Schloss Ricklingen, although obviously I had my own ulterior motives.'

Churchill sipped his brandy, looking over the top of his glasses in that very typical way of his.

'Your ulterior motives, Philip ?' he said.

'Ah, yes, rather trickier, that. Let me show you something.'

On the long table in front of Churchill, he unrolled a big map of the area north-west of Hanover, a smaller version of the one which had hung on the wall in the Operations Room at Bovingdon. Taking a slim, silver, propelling pencil from his inside pocket, he pointed at the map.

'Here, as you see, is Seelze. The factory complex over here on the west.'

'Go on,' Churchill said, taking out a fresh cigar and lighting it.

'Now over here, on the eastern side of Seelze, are the marshalling yards – by the way, we've got some rather good snapshots of those. Come in useful when the RAF is ready to go in with the new bombers.'

'Be a while before that happens,' Churchill growled.

'Here, just east of the town, outside Letter, is the factory which makes the Luftwaffe's bomb-sights, Gebrüder Hermann Kleefeld GmbH. From here, bomb-sights are sent to every aircraft factory in Germany. By road, along the autobahns, by barge along the canals, by rail from the marshalling yards. Ideally situated to get them where they have to be, as quickly as it is possible to ship them. We couldn't wait until we had the bombers to go over and flatten it – by that time half of the cities of England would be piles of rubble. But we had to take it out. The trouble was, of course, that it was not only well-guarded, but linked to the Gestapo headquarters at Seelze with automatic alarm systems.'

'I see,' Churchill said.

'I thought you would,' the Chairman smiled.

'You wanted a diversion. While they were all chasing Smith and his – ah, savages – ?'

'Another team was putting enough high explosive under the Kleefeld factory to ensure it would not function again this side of Christmas.'

'And ?'

'It went sky high last night,' the Chairman smiled. 'At almost exactly the same time as the Gestapo *Hochhaus* in Schloss Ricklingen !'

Churchill nodded, pushed his glass forward. 'I think I'll take another one of those,' he said. 'Your people got out safely ?'

'Easy as pie,' was the reply. 'Smith's people had so effectively cut off communications that they had a very easy run. In fact, the chappie who led them said they could have walked in wearing bowler hats and striped trousers for all the trouble they had. Smith and his men had turned Seelze into an island by blowing all the bridges into the town. They'd destroyed the telephone exchange, set fire to the Gestapo headquarters in the town. On top of that, when they blew up the *Hochhaus* at Ricklingen, all military communication between Hanover and the rest of Germany was put out of action.'

'Have we had a report on the bomb-sight place?' Churchill asked.

'87 per cent destruction,' the Chairman said. 'Oh, by the way, there was one funny story: when Miller was recce-ing the marshalling yards, he flushed the Kleefeld team. They were using a platelayer's hut and he just walked in on them. They gave him some fairy story, fed him a cup of coffee. He left, and they got on with the job. Didn't know he was British, obviously. Just as Miller didn't know they were. Duty Officer spotted it in the reports.'

'None of them suspected anything?'

'Nothing. Oh, and that reminds me,' the Chairman put in. 'This fellow Miller. In prison, apparently. Smith asked if we could put in a good word on his behalf.'

'Suspension of sentence, you mean?'

The NSE chief nodded. 'I imagine he meant something like that.'

'Hmph,' said Winston Churchill. But he was smiling.